S0-BEA-313

The Vision of Thady Quinlan

The Vision of Thady Quinlan

by Michael M. Mc Namara

CROWN PUBLISHERS, INC.   NEW YORK

HOUSTON PUBLIC LIBRARY

74-080350

R01158 79799

© 1974 by Michael M. Mc Namara
All rights reserved. No part of this book may be reproduced
or utilized in any form or by any means, electronic or mechanical,
including photocopying, recording, or by any information storage
and retrieval system, without permission in writing from the publisher.
Inquiries should be addressed to Crown Publishers, Inc.,
419 Park Avenue South, New York, N.Y. 10016.
Library of Congress Catalog Card Number: 73–91520
Printed in the United States of America
Published simultaneously in Canada by General Publishing Company Limited
Designed by Shari de Miskey

*For Mary,
Who Gave Me All
the Hope*

1

Bonsha Quinlan

I, BONSHA QUINLAN, come before anyone. I don't want to hear who's sick or dying or gone. I paid my money for this hard hospital bed and all that goes with it. And by God I'll get the worth of every pound. I broke my back for each farthing, and no one can take that from me, not even heaven and . . . God forgive me and keep me from all harm! Jesus, mercy! I was just rattling on!

An hour ago they began their preparations for Extreme Unction. The candles, the white cloths, and the bowls of water, all laid neatly beside my bed. But it won't be hard for me, making this Confession. I've had the priest down here every night. Holy Viaticum, food for the journey. I'm as ready now as I'll ever be. Just sit around and wait, as the fellow says. There's nothing at all left to do, except maybe sip a little more of the lemon they've put against my mouth. Tomorrow, if I make it until then, there will be that light soup I've come to like. Yes, that's something to look forward to. Jesus, what I wouldn't give for a fag, though. Maybe Kevin will light one up and give me a quick drag when he and the rest of the family come in to see me later on. The small straw left after the harvest. There were times when I'd puff away as much as three packs of fags in a damn sitting. Ah, for just one of the dirty things right now. Not for its taste, really, but to hold on to the time. I can't see why they just don't give me whatever it is I ask them for. Didn't they tell me that it was only a matter of days for me? I could go off in the bat of an eye. Then why in the name of Jesus must I linger here without a last bit of enjoyment? A drop of whiskey and a fag would make their lot easier and put me on my way. You'd think that I wasn't prepared to go, by the way they treat me. Five Holy Communions this week and anointed twice! Those doctors must be atheists. They have to be. Especially if they're anything like the nurses around here.

You wouldn't believe the likes of these women they have as hospital help. They're another breed of people altogether. Bending over, showing their arses up to the black part. I swear I saw one this morning and she didn't have as much as a pair of knickers to cover her hole. And when they change you, they have their big fleshy jugs right in your face so that you can't breathe without practically taking a bite out of the bloody things. If I was a well man and a year or two younger, they'd be up on me like whelps in heat, putting their auld things under the sheets to me. Whores, the lot of them. I know. I knew their likes in England when I was there. Black ones, white ones, and yellow ones. And half of them not able to utter a word of the King's English except "short time" and "fast one for a quid." I knew them. These are no different, except that they have more of a disinfectant smell.

Thank God, I never raised my children like that. No, I was the strict one. I kept them in line. And I won't let up after I've gone neither. It's soft living that makes for sin and sloth. Idle hands, as the old saying has it. Give an inch and they'll take a foot. So I'm giving no rope.

They'll all be down to have a last look at me before long. All except Thady. Paddy will come back, but not Thady. Not after all them letters and cards and God-knows-what he sent me over the years, and I not able to put two words together to answer him. And even if I was, I don't think I'd have done it. He ran off out of this place with nothing but curses on his tongue. Spitting vomit in my face, after all the hardship and sweat it took to raise him. But he paid dearly for his temper to me that day. Ten years of exile. Ten years is a long time. But he's a better man for it, I'll have to admit. He's reached the heights and left the weak and crippled behind. It was I taught him all he knows. But I suppose he'll never give me that credit. Oh no, children have little respect for their parents. They just feed off them like lamper eels.

Take Paddy. A good worker, but he spent every penny on fags and porter. Mind you, I liked the drop myself, but never to the excess that he took it. Off with him to England, for reasons I won't stoop to mention. And I having to fund him the money. Married a sow of woman who's brought him nothing but children and more children. But he's too tomfool to know his misery. He wasn't like Thady, who saw all the colors of the rainbow at one glance. Paddy knows only that twenty shillings make a pound and that if you've got a fiver you're well-off. The poor fool. But where ignorance is bliss, I suppose, as they say. I'd like to see him before I go, though. Paddy and me had good old times on the river. Fights, blood, curses—but good old times. He was a whale of a worker, Paddy was. There was no shortage of money when he took the sandcot up by Plassey, that's for sure. Kevin is like him in that way, but he has even less sense. He's just an auld idiot. He'll never amount to anything.

And the girls, Maud and Sadie. What can you say about women? I ask of you, except that they're born, they're taken to bed, and then put at the stove for the rest of their days, when the warm smell of them turns to slime in your nostrils. Two I had; one now married and out like a cow from the prod. Married to a gett who spends his whole year in England and then comes home like a monk on holidays to get as much as he can. But he can't fool me. I know the look in the eye and the big show of affection in front of me and Chrissie, my wife. He's not pulling the wool over my eye, that Jimmy. No, sir. He's getting his hole over there in England. You can be sure of that.

What is there to say about Sadie? She's only good as a servant about the house. She never goes to a dance. She never has a court with a fella or ever has had one! She's an auld dope. Instead of being out there every night, after work and when the house is cleaned, dancing her arse off. It's her own fault. She's like her mother. Stuck around the fireplace getting sooty and long-faced. It was for the same thing that I almost went back to England after I coming home from there, years ago. Home was a grand place to come to every now and again. But *be* there for more than a fortnight and you wanted to scream like a bloody madman. The money was running out. Chrissie sitting by the fire holding onto her precious Thady like he was gold coin. Don't touch him for this! Don't touch him for that! God forgive me, I was fit to be tied. I don't think that I was so much against the child as I was against her holding on to him, and mollycoddling him at every turn. I swore that if I'd get work, I'd stay and put an end to that nonsense. It wasn't a week when I met one of the sandcotters down at Deegan's having a pint. He put me on his boat, and I knew the jetties and coves of that river until a year or so ago. But women are strange and wily when they want to be. I never quite got the better of her. Oh, we fell back in together again; where else do you think the other

4

children came from? But she drew Thady closer to her all the time. That isn't to say that I didn't get him on my own every now and again and knuckle the head off him. I might have wronged him, I'll admit, but the little fucker, God forgive me, thrived on it. You'd catch him watching you at times out of those dark sallow eyes of his and wonder if he was going to murder you when your back was turned. But you couldn't help being proud of him at times. Always head of his class. A decent oarsman. I watched him cough up blood on the planks one night after a regatta. Of course, he never knew I was watching. Always winning prizes. But as for river work he was useless. He couldn't do a bloody thing right.

There were times when I had to think back and ponder what I did to Thady. There was that day he brought home the two white rabbits from the marketplace and put them on the chair next to me. "Look, Da," says he, "I'm going to raise these and make a fortune for myself. I have a hutch from Finn Keough, and I can pick up cabbage leaves from the marketplace every Wednesday and Saturday. And I got the two of them for only five bob." Up I stood. I grabbed hold of them two clawing, squealing things, and out with me into the lane. I threw them as hard as I could into Mackey's field, and away with them like wildfire. "Now," said I, "if you ever bring anything like that into the house again, there's where it'll go, as sure as God's in heaven." Do you think he cried? Your arse! He just stood there defying me. I belted him across the kisser, but he just tightened his thin little lips and walked away toward the field. I got to thinking later. It wasn't the fucking rabbits, God forgive me, that made me so mad. But, Jesus, five shillings thrown out the window like it was water. Five shillings that could buy bread or a bit of beef or a good pig's head. Or ten or twelve pints in those days. But as I said, I might have wronged him. It was his mother's bloody fault, giving him the money. She had the notion that I was still in England and the money was coming out of my arse. But wronged or no wronged, it was my place as a father to do as I saw fit. You'd want to see my auld fella before me. I don't think that two hundred words passed between us all during his life. Not even to tell me off! Jesus, you'd be sitting there, not doing a thing, when, God in heaven this night, his boot would catch you right between the haunches and you'd be sent flying. Do you think I ever stood up and asked him the reason? I'd have been taking my sacred life in my hands. But it's all gone now. Thady nor myself are the worse for it. He's riding high.

What's that? Oh, it's them. The whole slua. The wife, Sadie, Maud, and Kevin. And Finn Keough with a fag in his mouth. They mustn't have caught him with it on the way in. Grand. He'll give me a drag. I can almost taste the smoke in my lungs. Like the grand feeling of mounting up. Jesus, mercy! Confound my impurities!

2

Thady

THE TRAIN SLOWED gradually as the tracks and signals and station houses rose on all sides, moving us like some ornate main celebrant into the increasing density of Limerick Station. Past the county council schemes, the paint dried hard on their sills and windows. New buildings sprouting up between the blackened walls of the old city. Was that large protruding hulk of steel and glass there before I left? I couldn't remember. Some old reliable signs: O'Donnell's Sausages; Ryan's Condensed Milk; Whitbourne Cheese. The surface may have adjusted, but here the heart never lets its overcoat become its landlord. There they were as always, railroad men standing between the tracks, waving greasy hands like children. Linesmen tipping teaspoonfuls of gravel on their broad shovels, all smiles in their ragged jerseys and wet Woodbines. A grand life.

We moved slowly under the canopy and into the darkness. The train squealed. On another platform a man was leaving, fleeing, as I had, to the dark corners where loneliness is a way of life, but at home the image expands. Two melodeon players and a fiddler tore their hysteria from worn instruments. The man had packages under his arms. Waterford crystal, Connemara marble. Linen, perhaps, as white as his soul. Taking out gifts. Before, one brought them back. A strange new balance. If only it could be determined, beyond the customs' rule, what it was we took out and brought back in our veins. An eternity of weights and measures of the soul. And maybe a final yellow chalk mark to say that we were in perfect balance. Owing nothing; taking less.

And now I was coming home. Omaha. New York. London. Crew. Hollyhead. Irish Sea. Dun Leery. Naas. Curragh. Limerick. A spiral boring back into the soil, with me as the diamond bit. Home for my father's funeral. The telegram wasn't vague. *Father dead. Come if you can.* Signed by my mother. I had carried the telegram across the parched April lawns of the university where I am called professor by some who take the time to salute. Into the dean's office. Kind Herb Jonassen looked up from his cluttered desk. *Why certainly, Thady, take the time and go back. Don't worry about a thing here. I'll take care of everything.* I thanked this generous friend and walked slowly toward my rooms.

My father's death had come as no shock to me. Finn Keough, former school friend, eternal correspondent and recorder of deaths, had made it clear in his last letter, its crumpled contents still in my pocket.

Dear Thaed,
    Your old man's had it. The boyo's got him. I was down to see him last night. I mentioned you. He called

---

you his wild scholar. Is there any chance you could get back? He was a hard man. But God help us. Remember the night he caught me with his boot instead of you? A terrible man altogether.

Write or wire on the dot.

Do cairde,

Finn

Terrible man with knotted fists now tightened for good. Frozen to strike no more. Laid out by young nurses of girls whose voices rasp of the night's frolics. Oh, I remember you, terrible man, whose spurts of flaming anger roared out of the pores of you, a vessel of old dog's anger.

I walked through the railway stile. A shriveled civil servant, all smiles, all hope, carried my two suitcases, his dirty embroidered suit torn and snotted at the cuffs. Across the gray emptiness of the station. A few C.I.E. secretaries visible through the glass panes. In the same corner as years ago the tin-imprinting machine stood idle. A sign read *Out of Order.* Perhaps it was ludicrous to print our threepenny affections on a strip of tin, but we used to. It was the only permanency we knew.

Out under the last arch and into the bright sunlight. A courtyard of cars and taxis and one pony tied to the railings. I stood, letting the warmth touch my face, becalmed on this platform above all the bustle below.

"Will you want a taxi, sir?" the wizened face under the railway cap looking up at me.

"Hell, no! I want a sidecar."

"Oh, lord, nobody uses them anymore. It's all taxis now, sir."

"Fuck taxis. Isn't there a jarvey left?"

"One. But he just hauls suitcases."

"Get him. There's a pound in it for you."

My servant of the moment running off to the side of the building. Returning seconds later, a thin smelly little man in tow. Eyes half-open. Thick lines of grease under the slits. His name was Joe, and I knew him. A man fawned on by many sisters. Who gave him the white collar and shined boots on a Sunday for mass, before they died one by one. Leaving him in the defecation of himself.

"Joe Mulanney!" At the words his eyes emerged out of the tired skin.

"God, sir, who do I have here?"

"Quinlan. Thady Quinlan. I used to buy apples from your sisters long ago."

"Oh, Jesus Christ! Thady Quinlan. Thady Quinlan. God, I wouldn't know you." Then the darkening, falling, curdling of reality. "I'm awfully sorry for your troubles, Thady. He was a grand man, your father. You look like him in the eyes. I'm very sorry."

How many more returning had heard the same incantations over and over? And I would hear them again until they became as normal to each day as the rain. Yet they had a strange soothing cadence beyond their meaning.

"Where to, Thady? The house?"

"No, not yet, Joe. I'm in need of a little courage. What pub do you think Finn Keough would be in?"

"Deegan's."

"Are you sure?"

"He was baptized there!"

"Deegan's, then."

Up on the staired cart. Perched high as in childhood when we rode to Dooneas of a Sunday. The children stacked in mortal dread beside a short fat jarvey who farted constantly with the horse's tail rising to emit the same green smells. And the dung fell into the low shelf of the car, and we sat clustered together avoiding its wet smooth mounds. In the front car, my father's voice ringing out his "Rose of Clonmel" as we galloped under the dark trees and out into the sunlight of birds and flies. And the blackthorn branches tore at our skins, but we were immune to pain at the thoughts of the falls and water and minnows and eel fry waiting to be caught and carried home in jam jars. But a mile beyond Larkin's Cross, he fell from his high place among the women and into the grass, his leg under him. And because he was he, they turned back to the first pub. The children were put on benches to sip their lemonades and watery cordials until the cold air chilled us in our flimsy cotton shifts. My father's eyes were dazed from the drink and pain, but he laughed and laughed, spilling his Guinness over my trousers.

"Would you like me to take a back street, Thady."

"Straight through town."

"Right you are."

We were in O'Connell Street now. Dashing past cars. Lorries and horns. A man rolling his bicycle along the footpath for safety. At Carlton's Pool Rooms the players in their yellow skin gave us the stale glance. Cigarette butts in mouths. Sucking down the brown juices. They had longer hair than before but still as dirty. People pouring out of Osmond's Stores where once they sold only First Communion suits and you were obliged to stand in your skin as little old ladies glanced at your balls and made remarks as to family resemblance. We were passing the lights. A man stood out from the path. His young face coiled in hate. He raised his hand, the middle finger pointed straight at us.

"Arra fuck off out of that." Joe raised the whip to strike.

"What's the matter with him?" I asked as the man ran into the crowd.

"Ah, he's daft. He saw that you were a Yank, and he blames America for the war."

"Vietnam?"

"No, no. The First World War."

"But, Jesus, he must be in his twenties. He wasn't even thought of then, for heaven's sake."

11

"But sure that's it. I'm telling you he's mad."

Finally, after the parade of streets, we arrived at the corner pub below the Bishop's Bridge. Joe refused a drink before his supper but promised to have one later on if I'd leave it for him. He would hear of nothing but to drop my bags off at the house on his way back to the station to meet the last train from Dublin. "Always a lot of suitcases on that one," he confided.

I stood in the concrete doorway of Deegan's. A small push and the latch clicked open. Two soot-faced men who smelled of the docks were coming out. They stood apart from me, afraid that their raggedy clothes would touch my raincoat. I pushed past them into the light. The stools along the bar were crowded. Laughter and spitting. Ferret eyes along the barrels and in the nooks searching out my face. The girls behind the bar looked up from their skimming of pints and filling of mugs. Three rough-looking men stared at my reflection in the mirror.

A face came out of the jakes. A thick-set frame that hobbled as it dragged a heavy leg behind it. A head as large as that of an ox, wild curls sticking out like thistles. He didn't look up, but removed a dirty white towel and togs from a stool and hoisted himself awkwardly onto the cushion. The head settled into its white baneen. I moved through the sawdust, the whispers closing in after me like dust on baked summer roads. I was behind him. I stared at his reflected image in the mirror. At first it glared insolence at catching my eye but broke to reveal the big white teeth of childish friendship.

"Oh, Jesus, Mary, and Joseph, if it isn't the son of the parish come back from the dead! How in the name of J are you, Thady Quinlan?"

"Fit as a fiddle and mad for it!"

"It's like you, Thaed."

"And how's Finn Keough?"

"In there with all the other botts, Thaed. In there."

Finn grabbed a youngster on the next seat, lifting him effortlessly then dropping him on the floor. "Get the fuck out

---

12

of that, you little maggot. Let a man who has traveled from the other side of the world sit down. He was drinking porter on that stool when you were pissing in your nappy. Wait till I see your auld fella. Drinking at your age. Get on out of that."

The lad scurried off toward the back door. Looking with hatred nourished by thirst. Finn's demon eyes following his every step.

"Have you ever seen the likes of that? Not old enough to hold it themselves and sucking like maneens on jars."

"How about ourselves, Finn, at Sparling's long ago?"

"Yes, but we had the decency to hide behind the trees in case we were seen."

"True."

"So tell me, Thaed, when did you get in?"

"An hour ago. I had Joe Mulanney drive me down."

"Christ Almighty! Joe's a fucking madman. You're lucky you're alive. It's a good thing you're a parish man. A week ago yesterday he was arrested by the guards for pissing in the letter box of the parish credit union."

"What?"

"It seems they refused him a few quid that afternoon, so he decided to take revenge."

"Things never change."

"Like your auld fella, Thaed. He never changed."

Finn's face turned away. He had liked my father as those outside the windows see the shopkeeper as a man forever joking, breaking toffee, or tossing the pennies with a jingle. Never seeing the contrivance that makes the face gyrate for public mirth. Finn and he had been close when silence was all that passed between my father and me. Finn talked to him for me. Finn laughed at his jokes or hung on his stories of the river. Now beckoning to the girl at the register. "Two tall dark ones here, Bridie," he said.

"Let me get them, Finn."

"Not at all."

"I'm sorry about the blackdog. I know you liked him. *My* memories aren't the kindest."

"I know, Thaed. It's none of my business. But he was a good old friend to me when I was growing up. Your feelings are your own, and you had your reasons. You should know, though, where he's at. He's at Thomond's deadhouse. You know that it was the boyo that got him?"

"Heart?"

"Yes."

The waitress brought the draughts. Her blue country eyes caught mine for a second. She smiled.

"Nice bit of stuff." Finn nodding at the girl's backside as her mini stretched over her heavy thighs. "But stupid as a gett. Up from Dingle, where they sleep with pigs. But a nice arse."

"Is it clean?"

"Her arse?"

"No, you crazy bastard. Her, I mean."

"Hell, I wouldn't know. I suppose she washes as much as the rest of us when the need comes around. If she has a stink, I'll bet it's one of good beer slops mixed with an occasional drop of whiskey. Am I getting to you, Thaed? You're awfully green at the gills."

"No. But you're trying awfully hard, you prick!"

"Ha ha! Just seeing if you still have the weak stomach for dirt."

That was the chant from long ago. *Did your sister Maud wash your arse tonight, Thady? Did Sadie dry it? And was a little powder left for your balls?* Having attentive sisters and boiling water was a definite liability. Cleanliness had a suspicious stench around our laneway. Too much cleanliness, Brother Rogan used to say. It is the sin of the Americans. Too much water and soap. Man's striving to attain the infinite purity of God. Americans are drenched and scoured animals of the forest, agile and nubile as beasts. But *beasts,* not men. Beasts whose only ecstasy is that of self. And I had asked if it was not in keeping with God's will to be a searcher after purity, whether it be physical or spiritual. And the prying into the hues and twists went on for days. Deciphering some austere God's will from the generalities of His edicts was a teen-age obsession of mine. I had tried to lull it to sleep over the years, but time had left me uneasy at the end of a queer tide with soundless stirrings beneath. I had tried to ignore its turible odors and melodious chants, placing it in its real perspective of childhood. Sometimes I warred against it, but as a mad dog is not dissuaded by the clomp of jarring rock against its flesh, it returned to plague me in new lights. *Non serviam.* The syllables so easy and so pompous but, in truth, all part of the same magic. The cure being the very disease. I remembered the words, the chants, and the music. The soft cadence, reaching into the thump-throb inside, enchanting the soul into sweet servitude. Easters running ahead of the laments. Tenebrae. The yellow wax of the candles. The fissure of light and the aroma of exotic incense. The child words of Christmas breathed through the straw stables, reminding the lingering longing soul of the infinite benevolence of the child monarch. *He lies mid the beasts of the stall, Who is Maker and Lord of us all.*

A loud clanging came from above us. The television screen simply said "Angelus," and the bells rang over the heads of the crowd. The old men held their caps on their knees. The younger ones looked embarrassed. The gongs played on. Finn stirred in his own contemplation. When it was over, the noise thickened in curses and loud laughter. Words, sounds, smells, abrasive touches caving in to devour the ominous regimentation of the bell.

"So how's the sex life, Thaed, now that you're single and carefree?"

"Could be better."

"Sure, it always could be better. I bet you have all kinds of college stuff traipsing at your heels."

"Dreamer."

15

"None at all?"

"Some. An odd piece of ass joins the faculty every fall. But I usually lose out to some jock from the P.E. department by Thanksgiving."

"No young stuff?"

"That would be the end of my career."

"But sure, life is all a delicious chance. Didn't you tell me about some little thing you had earlier this year? You mentioned her in a letter a few months ago. I got the impression that it was serious."

"It was beginning to get that way."

"What happened?"

"A temporary idyll. A rite of spring. Like years ago up Plassey with the girls from Clare Street and the Ennis Road. Remember?"

"God be with the youth of us, Thaed. I often think back. I say to myself that we could have lasted forever up there with the water and the sun and the grass and the swans."

"I have never forgotten it. It was Paradise—a place separate from all the pain. I'm going to go back up there before I leave."

"Anyway, you were saying about this girl you had."

"Kathy was her name. I liked her for awhile."

"You were into it?"

"Regularly."

"Hard man!"

"It was becoming too serious. I had to call a halt to it."

"She wanted marriage?"

"That was the general idea."

"What stopped you?"

"The freedom, I suppose. The tightening suffocates me. I was single for too long. I should have never gotten married in the first place."

"Yes, Thaed, but women will always look for permanency. You know that. And sometimes it isn't all that bad when you

---

16

can give them a good clout now and again to bring them to their senses. You're a successful man. You're in good shape. Shit, if I had all you've got, I'd be in the market for a wife tomorrow. Fuck, I can't even find one of my old courts from long ago. They're married and fat with chubby children and consumptive husbands. If nothing else, you've produced legal offspring—someone to carry on the tradition."

"That's not saying too much, I can tell you."

"How is the lad, by the way?"

"Healthy. I visit him a few times a year. He'll be five in a few weeks. I'll get to see him then. But that's poor consolation."

"But look at me! A bloody cripple taking what I can get down on the Dock Road. If I have any offspring, they're not the ones that'd look me in the eye on a Sunday after mass."

"Dock Road?"

"What did the Dock Road always mean? Prostitutes. Shit, they've been here since Ginkell."

"When we were growing up?"

"Certainly. They weren't as clean then. Spotless as a tin whistle now. Swanks go down there. Jaguars and everything. Some even have rooms at the Leinster Hotel. Three pounds alone wouldn't get you five minutes."

"You're a hard man. What would the Order of Saint Jerome have to say if they heard you?"

"What they don't know won't trouble them. But I didn't tell you. I'm a prefect in charge of the Blessed Maria Goretti section. Religion has honed my appreciation of lust. Made a connoisseur out of me."

"You'll never make it to heaven."

"It's making it in both places that's my goal. The religion is marvelous insurance."

"Too much perverted Pascal and not enough drink. Let's have another round."

A new girl began to operate the beer cocks. Her hair was brown, her eyes dark and set deep in her pale skin. She wore

17

a white apron. As she moved, attending each stool in order, her bosom swayed heavily beneath the light blouse. She caught my stare more than once. She smiled and pointed to my glass. Finn noticed my interest.

"Fine stuff that, isn't it?"

"Who is she?"

"She comes from the Abbey. You probably wouldn't remember her. Agnes Clancy is her name."

"Raef's sister?"

"No. Another Clancy. She lives on the corner of Sheep Street. Her marriage name was Gilligan, before the fuck of a husband she had ran off and left her. I'll introduce you. We're very great."

"Fine."

Finn gestured to her. She smiled, finished filling a glass, and came down the bar. Her scent reached out from the sour odors all around. Teeth moist and inviting. Her body damp and supple. Pursing her lips, she said, "Another two, Finn?"

"Right, Agnes." Finn a little shy. "A tall one for my royal guest, Thady Quinlan. Thady, this is Agnes Clancy, the most beautiful woman in the parish, in all of Ireland, for that matter."

"Go on, you big rogue. Don't mind him, Thady. He says that to every woman, from two to toothless." She blushed for an instant, then looked at me. "I'm sorry for your troubles, Thady. I knew your father. He often sang over there at the piano. He was a very nice man, God rest him."

Her face showed a genuine sadness. Not the kind that gives condolence and asks when you're going back, in the next breath. She touched my hand in sympathy; then, feeling self-conscious, she moved toward the faucets to fill our drinks. Finn put his weight on the good leg. "Be right back, Thady," he said. "Have to take a slash."

A man at the bar was throwing a gabardine over his shoulder and wiping his lips on the cuff. He faltered slightly, then barged through the crowd spilling beer on women and old men. Loud curses everywhere. One old hag reached out to grab him by the trousers. She missed. He was out of the confusion and into the hallway. Recriminations in hot pursuit. Everybody wiping themselves. Suddenly his face was at the window. Then his arm raised in bent fashion to tell all present that it was up their ballyhaunis. He was gone.

"Isn't he a terror?" Agnes wiping the dregs from the counter and positioning the beers on cardboard coasters.

"Brave, too."

"Oh, he'll be back. It never fails. Then there'll be holy murder."

"Times haven't changed. There was always one like him here. Do you know Gulla Franklin?"

"Oh, don't I know him! He's a holy terror."

"Still the same gas man."

"How long have you been gone, Thady? To America, I mean."

"Ten years. I left when I was eighteen. I went to England first, when the old man ran me out of the house. Then a relative took me to New York."

"But you're not still in New York?"

"No. I live in Nebraska now—Lincoln. A cesspool of degeneration."

"You dislike it that much?"

"Listen, I'd like to buy you a drink if you'd let me?"

"I'd love to, Thady, but it would never do. We're not allowed to until we're off. But I'll have a lemonade with you on my break, if you like. I'll be on it in a few minutes when Bridie relieves me."

"I'll move over by the window."

"Fine, Thady."

I carried the pints to an empty space between the Guinness barrels. A dog shuffled to make way. Several men eyeing me out of caked slits of eyes. Some still wondering who I was. Thinking

19

that I'd be good for a free jar if only they could remember when our paths had crossed. Finn was back.

"Jesus, I see you lost no time with Agnes. She's nice now, Thaed. Don't forget that."

"Private stock?"

"Come on!"

"You don't mind if I talk to her?"

"Christ, Thady, stop right now. It's just that she's had her share of sorrow."

"A word unknown to me?"

"You have a hundred roads, Thaed. She has barely a foot-path."

"Finn, are you . . ."

"Shhh. Here she comes."

Agnes folded her apron and settled a gray tweed on her shoulders. Her dark hair was loosed from its clasp and fell across her breasts. She walked toward us.

"You two look like sour milk. Cheer up."

"We were waiting for your smile," I said. "Still just a lemonade?"

"That's all, Thady."

Finn twitched uneasily. He beckoned to a short oily man at the bar and then excused himself, saying that his friend had a few bob for him from the fourth race that afternoon. He'd be back in a jiffy.

"Have you been home yet, Thady?"

"No."

"The funeral is tomorrow, you know?"

"Is it?"

"That's what Finn says. He was down at the house earlier. Your brother Paddy is back from England. Maud and Sadie were in to pick up stout and whiskey about an hour ago."

"How did he die?"

"Finn didn't tell you?"

"Not exactly."

"Well, as far as I hear it, he just dropped off. They were all sitting by his bed, and he fell back with the rattles in his throat."

I suddenly saw him lying there, struggling to retain his life. That fierce, cruel old man whom I had considered eternal. He was dead. Disarmed forever. Not waiting threateningly at the end of our laneway for my return. I was free at last from his clutches. But I could not scour my mind of his memory. "Did they try to revive him?" I asked.

"It was too late, I guess."

"You mean that right there in the hospital they just considered it God's will and let it go at that?"

"But sure, Thady, when your time comes you have to go. There's no way to prevent that. We can't be living forever."

"No. But we sure as hell can delay death. That's what life is all about."

"Are you afraid of death, Thady?"

"Yes, I am. It's the end of life, and life is all there is. When you die there's nothing."

"You sound so sure of that."

"And you? How do you feel? Do you feel that some Omnipotent Creator, in gray beard, will come heralding down the skies to escort your immortal soul into Paradise?"

"Thady, you sound like a catechism. No, I won't say that I disbelieve it. The truth is that I rarely give it a thought. I'm too busy during the day and too tired when I go home at night. I don't go around with the Ten Commandments in front of me, picking at every one and finding myself lacking here or gaining there. If there is a hereafter, I'll be prepared. If there isn't, I haven't let it come between me and my night's rest. My life isn't the best, but I have a roof over my head and food on the table. For that I am grateful."

"You never hope for something better?"

"I do, now and again."

"What?"

"Well, it would be nice to have a husband at home. Children around the house. A picture every so often. But it didn't work out that way, and I'm not fooling myself."

"That's all to life, then?"

"There are days when you're in black hell for awhile, then along comes some little brightness that softens you. Like this little break. I'm enjoying myself talking to you. So if tomorrow has another cross, I'll face that obstacle when I come to it."

Her face showed a madonna's strained sadness. Her fingers touched mine as I lit her cigarette. There was a sweet musk about her. Clean bosom and neck. She smelled like the young secondary girls of long ago. Her shoulders were light and moved with little-girl uncertainty.

There was a sudden commotion by the front door. Obscenities floating in all directions. *Up the Black and Tans. Your mother's arse. Fuck the Taoiseach, the blind auld whore.* A table overturned. Hands grabbing at throats to locate the usurper of the tranquillity. *A bollocks on Sinn Fein. Up the North.* Heads searching out on every lip the heresy of the strident voice. It seemed, however, to be coming from the largest man on the premises. Blackguards throttling everybody but this man who calmly sips his beer. Fists ready to draw blood.

"Jesus, Thady, I'm going in the back. There'll be bloody murder here in a munute."

"Lovely. We need a bit of sport, this dreary night."

"You'll be thinking sport, love, when the bottles start flying."

"Who's getting their ire up?"

"Take a quick look over there."

"The big man? He's not even moving his lips."

"He isn't. But look behind his back."

A quick glimpse of a familiar face. The little man of the gabardine coat and raised arm had returned to shout his taunts in the big man's shadow. Someone spotted him. He was dragged by the scruff, a small spider twitching above the hands that reached to tear him asunder. Hoisted over the crowd like a sacrificial toad. He beating on the heads of his indignant opponents with no surcease to his tongue's agility. Finn was beside me.

"We're going to have to save him or they'll tear his nuts off."

"What can we do?"

"Make as much noise and commotion as possible."

The warmth of the drink giving strength to the pale muscles. Tables over. Other friends of the little toad taking up the flank. The voices saying, "Oh, Jesus, I've bursted me shins." An old one screamed that someone had a finger in her knickers. But she smiled as she complained. Bottles struck obdurate skulls. The door swinging like an idiot as the less-than-stouthearted fled the stout and assorted bottles. A handful of sawdust was thrown in the foe's eyes. Screams of murder. *De-nut the little maggot.* But he ferreted his way under the legs. Pulling at available peckers and irritating friend and not-so-friendly. Farts wafting across the room like uneasy spirits. A grand melee with the blood at the nerve ends, and hearts on the cuffs to be split open on request. All about me beating the daylights out of each other. A vacant chair. A speech! I was in the mood for revolt. Up I jumped.

"Hear ye! Hear ye! Hell and damnation on the Republic. Fuck the revolution!"

Someone said, "Who in the name of Jasus is that?"

"Ah, he has a lovely speaking voice," said another.

To which I replied, "I am the curator of the Holy Oils. I package farts in jam jars for the black babies to be used in oxygen tents and for the control of riots. I am president of the movement to turn the bladders of rugby balls into French letters . . ."

Two bottles split above me in a blitz of response. "I'll tear that fucking Yank alive," a voice said. And a man whose purple veins resembled the silt-laden estuaries of the Boyne bore down on me. *All we need is a bollocks Yank to interfere in our business.* Hands reaching to halt this monster. Failing. The bull bore on. Almost on me. The last step. Suddenly, he fell face forward by the aid of twenty boots in the balls and a general rejuvenation of the fight. Finn withdrew his boot, his arm under mine.

"Let's get out of here before we're slaughtered."

"I had a ball."

"If we stay you'll have none."

Out through the back door. With smells of piss and overflowing jakes. Green-slimed walls. Old barrels stained in urine and birdlime. A man humming "The Rose of Tralee" as he relieved himself and smoked a fag. "Night to ye," he said casually. "Is there a singsong inside?" To which we replied nothing but bolted down the old gray mall. Like horses that have come out of the night, their foam and sweat drenching them in their urgency. Pretending that the devil himself had ahold of their tails.

"Well, Finn, I guess I'd better face the music."

"Do you want me to come with you?"

"No. There may be ructions."

"I heard that the house is full. Try to keep that temper in your pocket."

"I'll try."

"Godspeed. Come on over later, if you take a notion to. I'm dead on my feet. I'm going to eat a bit of grub and sleep off the drink."

"Maybe later, then."

"Right, Thaed."

Finn moved into the dark pall of the night. I watched his limping figure turn into the narrow lane that led to his house. Maybe I should have taken him with me, I thought. It was beginning to squall off by the Bishop's Bridge. Bitter April days here. Never change, I thought.

24

3

Agnes

WHEN FINN AND THADY LEFT, the crowd simmered down. Threats and curses soon turned to laughter and conversation with Bridie and myself throwing lashings of beer onto the counter. As we ran the empties under the cock, Bridie was close by me. "Wasn't he lovely?" she said.

"Who?"

" 'Who,' says she. The Yank, of course."

"He has a fine way of making a mess."

"Go on now, Agnes Clancy. You had the bright eye out for him."

"Oh, stop your romancing, Bridie. I just met him this evening."

"Is he married?"

"He was. But he's not now. He's divorced."

"Well, if you don't want him, you can put in a good word for me. I'd wrawk him into bed with me without a minute's hesitation, let me tell you that."

"Bridie, you're a holy terror."

"Like I said, if you don't want him . . ."

"Bridie! Sure I liked him. Wouldn't any girl? But you know he had about as much interest in me as the man in the moon."

"You keep talking like that and no man will give you the time of day. You haven't had one to keep you warm since that worthless husband of yours off and left you without a penny to your name. You can't be sitting around on your own for the rest of your days."

"But I can't be throwing myself at every man who comes into this place, either. Thady Quinlan has a lot on his mind to be thinking of coming to see someone like me."

"He can't have that much. I could see him watching your every move right here from the counter."

"Bridie!"

"I swear to God."

"Maybe it's a mother he needs in all his sorrow."

"A man looking for a mother doesn't look the way he looked at you. He had that fire in his eye."

"And on his tongue, by the looks of all the broken glasses and spilled slops out there."

"Would you want a man without fire and spit?"

"I don't need a man who destroys things. Now, Bridie, let's get this place cleaned up so's we can get out of here early tonight. My feet are killing me."

We collected the dirty glasses one by one. Some of the men said that the fight was great sport. Others said that a man like that ought not to be left alive. The house gradually drank its way toward closing time, talking violently for one side or the other. When the drink wore off, they would hardly be able to remember Thady's name. Thady Quinlan, I thought to myself as the last men were slamming the door behind them. What sort of man was he? Oh, he looked good. The fine, strong shoulders, dark curly hair, and that tanned yellowish color that the Yanks have to their skin. But what was he underneath? I thought of my own fellow, years before. His shining white teeth, the voice of him singing with the men on a Friday night, and his shyness when he was alone with me. Only one day to walk out the door to England, with all the plans in the world to bring me over in a few months. And then never to hear a word from him again. But of course I wasn't alone. I wasn't the first one whose husband left this place and wasn't seen sign nor light of since. But maybe it wasn't all their faults. Maybe we smothered them when we had them. And made kings and angels out of them when they were only ordinary men, I thought. Just then Bridie brought a fistful of glasses to be dried, and I hadn't time to think further.

We washed and polished glasses for over an hour. Bridie made great noise with the water, but you had to watch her when it came to the cleaning. She had a habit of passing over the stains at the bottom of the glass. Her scrubbing was robust but not always thorough. Anyway, we were all done by half-past ten, and as I shut the door behind me, I thought of how Mr. Deegan would have a fit tomorrow when he heard of the row and the broken chairs and glasses. Well, that would be another few bob out of my pay packet. But we need a little liveliness at times, I thought as I pressed the latch shut.

On the mall, squalls of rain burst across the road. I was frightened of the sudden noise and loneliness. Two men came out of the Abbey, and for a minute I thought it was Thady and Finn. I quickened my step to catch up with them, calling their names as I came by. But it wasn't them at all, just two lads from Saint Brendan's Boat Club making their way home. I excused myself, saying that they were the image of two friends of mine.

27

They nodded and smiled, thinking, I suppose, that I was a bit of fluff after their attention. They turned abruptly and were gone.

In Sheep Street, I passed a courting couple under the eaves of the corporation cottages. The girl muttered good-night as I turned the corner to face my empty house. How nice it would be, I thought, to have someone by the hearth waiting for you. To have a sup of tea on the hob. To be held close under the heavy blankets and imagine that life was all rosy and without pain. I had known times like that, but they were very short. The thing was that they left the longing for more or for the hope that they would come again. I began to feel a sadness creep into me at the doorstep. I pulled myself up and told myself what a romancer I was. And I having the cheek to accuse Bridie! I had a life to lead, and God in His goodness had seen fit to give me that instead of being down on the docks like other poor deserted creatures, without a roof over their heads. I had a lot to be thankful for. I closed the door against the rain with a hard push. The cheek of me, I said to myself.

4

Thady

HIGHER BRAZIL STREET could only be reached by maneuvering through a tapestry of short foul lanes and alleyways. As children we had found it difficult to direct anybody there. Often, to avoid the embarrassment of the stench rising from cabbage water mixed with the washday's bleach in the gutters, we would arrange to meet our friends at Mary's Street Corner or outside Saint Mary's Church. Still, we never felt that our street itself was less than a glorious haven of security from the bitter wind of the river below and the ugliness outside its four small houses and cobbled pavement. It had been set aside, years before my father's time, as the proud territory of rivermen bent on securing for themselves a place of solace and relief but, I suppose, more so, as a plot that defied all about it in its stoic independence. There were good times here, I had to admit, years broken only by the occasional chastisements not uncommon in all the other households. The deprivation of dignity lasted only as long as the hiding's sting on the arse and the treacle of the Reeve's toffee on the tongue, tendered by Sadie, my younger sister, whose compassion was well-deep, and who softened my father's every outburst, just as she followed him around the house gathering up his carelessly strewn clothes. The real pain had only come in the last years here. With the loss of childhood awe giving way to the ever-emerging assertion of self.

I could see the outline of the houses as I came out of a black lane. On many a winter's night, as I rushed home before ten o'clock to make the family rosary or forever rue the day, the shadows had frightened me. To be without fear of the supernatural is not to be Irish. I would conjure up a myriad of spectres reaching out of every crevice to cloak me into them. Wandering souls. Headless coachmen. Old crones' words from hob's half-firelight. But when the terror had reached its spiral of bewilderment within me, I would stop and talk to it. I would defy it to touch me. I would balance my small-child's reason against its vaporous claws. I would command its cup of fear to cease its enchantment. And it had worked. The walls took back their hands and let me pass. Even now, the beginnings of this terror. And my father part and parcel of that dead world, by reason of his going. My father finally one of them. Hard to comprehend. Easy to imagine their impotency—strangers laid out on beds with closed eyes, the pennies recently removed. But Bonsha Quinlan. No! Not dead by their standards. I hurried on toward the streetlight above our house.

The small whitewashed cottage showed no light from the windows, blanketed in the tradition of death. But the open half door threw its brightness into the lane. There must be crowds inside, I thought, to have the door open on this cold night. The noise of the talk and movement soon reached me as I drew closer. Bicycles were piled against the wall. An empty pram was moored by twine to the rainspout between our house and the next. A cat darted into the darkness. I paused to look into the old face of the laneway. Standing there I noticed the sudden quietness, a pause. Had something happened? My curiosity was soon sated. A voice had broken into song. Not irreverent; just part of the long ritual. Oh, they would be irreverent later, in their fun-for-all interpretations. Now the voice was clear. A riverman singing of his boat as his love. Whose crevices were caulked and whose womb bore fish and sand. And who scolded never a time. One of my father's songs. This man's gift to the prolongation of the agony. And now it began, the voice reedy, tremulous, lashing the wet and dark.

Oh, my boat can safely float in the teeth of wind
    and weather,
And outrace the fastest hooker between Galway
    and Kinsale.
When the black foam of the ocean and the white foam
    leap together,
How she rides in her pride, like a sea gull in the
    gale.
Oh, she's neat, oh, she's sweet; she's a beauty
    every line,
The "Queen of Connemara" is that bounding bark
    of mine.

The oily surface of the water below me shone under the moon. The rain had cleared, but the wind was still cold. Ten years away. How to walk in and become in a brief moment the man I was? But I was never that here, only a mindless boy. To tell of experience and change and see no connections in their eyes. To relate the stringed web of a life spent away and find no understanding. To carry my chalice of me intact, because all of the towns were fleeting twinkling lights insignificant by the far-reaching glare of this backward place where I was first given life in the calloused womb of long ago. In this cranny were all the judgments made. In my absence. And even before my very time.

I touched the half door. The latch raised, dropped, and brought me into the kitchen light. Faces looking up from everywhere. Voices whispering. Froth on old women's lips. Red brown sherry in some hands. Women at the stove. The crackle of sausage and rasher. The black kettle on the immaculate hob. A candle burning. Faces coming out of their sudden parchment. *A stranger? Bonsha's brother? No. No. Too young. He's a Yank. Oh, Jesus, it's . . .* A plaintive voice from down by the fire. A woman rushing toward me, mantled in years but still recognizable. All her letters. All her words. And now my mother, a slight woman in blue bib and tear-drenched face, the eyes swollen like wasp-stung flesh. Out of the glawm of the women and into my arms. The shuddering failing body grasped tightly. *Oh, Thaed, let me look at you. You haven't changed a bit. Oh, my son, after all these years you've come back. You'll be blessed for it. Your name was on his lips before he died. Before he went, Thady. Oh, loving Jesus, what am I going to do without him? What am I going to do?* I held her, supporting her weightlessness as her tears ran against my flesh and clothing. The women were all around us. *Let her cry it out, God love us.* And they laid their arms under her, carrying her toward the fire again. A man entered the room from the hallway and called to me. I went toward him. "She'll be all right," he said. "It's just the terrible ordeal. Come on in to the front room for awhile until the women calm her. Paddy and Kevin are in there with all the men."

The front room was in darkness except for the blazing fire and the yellow tapers burning on the mantelpiece. The same china dogs, the cavities of whose arses I'd often used as a hiding

---

place for pilfered change, stared down into the blackness. The man led me to the fireplace. Someone vacated a sugan chair, and I reached to lay my coat across it. Hands extended everywhere. *Welcome back. It's a sad homecoming.* A young blond man beside me. The hair wild. The shirt collars flaring out. Before I could call his face out of photographs and shape it back to that of an excited child, always eager, always generous, my brother Kevin took me in his arms, his kisses flooding my face and neck. The liquor on the breath. *How are you, Thaed?* I could see him better in the fire's light. One of my shirts. The collars not buttoned down. The striped tie knotted in a shiny bulk. He began to sob. One of the men took him to a chair and his shoulder fell against the hob. A silence. The man across the light rose unenthusiastically from his staring into the flames. When his face turned toward mine the skin was taut and savage. My brother Paddy's hand came up slowly as if to strike. For a terrifying instant I thought that it would. Instead, it just hung there in the darkness. I reached and held it. The skin was hard like splintered wood, the grip loose. He moved my hand mechanically for a few seconds, then dropped it.

"How are you, Thady?" I saw his eyes look about him. The men were watching every move.

"Good, Paddy."

"The trip?"

"Tiring. And yours?"

"That damn ferry never changes."

"I was lucky; I had a berth. I slept on the way over."

"Oh." His face toward the fire. "Better sit down. No use standing there. Take a weight off."

As I settled into the chair, he began to toy with the poker, opening the faults of the coals and watching their blue flames gush into the red heat. He, the secondborn, encountering me, the first. The play, the dance. Paddy and I had never been close. We had tolerated each other in the same hive. Growing out toward different skies. I was still at the secondary when Paddy

---

33

finished Griffin Lane Primary and went on the river with my father. He had often discouraged me then, the white shillings in his hand on a Friday, a Gold Flake dangling from his mouth, saying, Thaed, when are you going to get enough sense and put the real things first? Them Brothers aren't going to put anything but airs in your head. I had listened and thought on that, but it always seemed that my mother or sisters happened to come to the rescue in time. To them the river meant toil. Education was the silver ticket to freedom and caste. My father and brother did the work. I delivered the sand after school and on Saturdays. But that was where it ended. Of course, Paddy was paid and could court the girls, while I, his senior, settled for the back seat of the Atheneum Cinema of a Sunday. The schoolgirl beside me having paid her own way. So it all had its compensations and balances, I suppose.

"What are you doing over now, Paddy?" I said. He didn't respond immediately. I thought at first that his silence was an insult. But suddenly his head came up out of the stupor.

"Sorry," he said. "I was off somewhere. What was it, Thady?"

"Your job now. Are you still at KLNKO, the ball-bearing company?"

"Lord, no. I left there a long time ago. Didn't Mama write you?"

"I must have forgotten."

"I have my own business. Nothing big. Small contracts."

"Construction?"

"Yes. That'd be what the Yanks call it. Building, labor, construction—different words. Same pain in the arse."

A man came out of the kitchen holding a tray laden with black pints. He handed Paddy the first. I reached and took one for Kevin, now sitting up and watching the faces in the firelight. My own drink felt cool against the palms. Someone had finally introduced the American coldness.

Paddy took the poker he was holding and reddened it over

the flames, then rammed it into his dark Guinness. The steam arose, wrapping him in mist. He touched the glass to his lips. He nodded at my drink. I refused the riverman's custom.

"Never heat it in the States?" he said.

"No. Beer is different there."

"No Guinness?"

"Yes, but almost fifty cents a half pint."

"Fifty . . ."

"About four shillings."

"Shit. That's not much different than here. Do you drink it at all?"

"I used to at first. But now at parties it's always vodka or gin. A martini or a gimlet."

"Women's drinks, you mean?" The bastard. He had the old man's way of direct gall.

"I'd like to see you walk home, Paddy, after two or three of them."

He laughed. Knew that my ire was up. His main intention from the start. Now equal for the moment. He would begin to talk at this point. I remembered the game. He had scars on the arms from his youngest days to remind him. Even sandcot men took mockery with a dim eye. He looked directly at me for the first time.

"You're a professor, we hear," he muttered into his drink.

"Just an assistant professor."

"You mean like an apprentice plumber?" Again he was after my hide.

"No. Not like that. There are various levels. Assistant, associate, and full. I'm at the beginning. It will take time and politics to climb the list."

"Just like a fucking plumber, then, like I said."

"Well, if you really need an analogy, yes. It is an apprentice stage. Except that to become even an assistant requires a doctorate. That means at least eight years of training at the university." He needed that, I thought.

"An-al-ogy? Boy, Thaed, you weren't using those words when you left here. They never swear like that here in Higher Brazil Street. You must be a walking dictionary, these days."

"Paddy, I teach every day. Those words are part of my vocabulary. I'm sorry, but Christ, you learned those terms up at the Brothers' secondary." Too late and I knew it!

"I wouldn't know. I never went there."

He turned to talk to a man behind him. A woman came from the kitchen. Where's Thady? she said. Over there. I waved. She was Mrs. Quinn from next door.

"Hello, love," she said, leaning down and kissing my face. "The years haven't changed you a bit."

"Oh, that's questionable."

"Here. Your mama wanted you to have this. It will fill up the sorrow. It's going to be a long night." She laid a linen cloth across my lap and settled the plate in the hollow of my thighs. The strong aroma caught my nostrils before I could distinguish the items of food. Fat thick-cut rashers. Black pudding made from pungent minces of the intestines. Blood pudding, or packet, set to the side, the milk of its stew soaking down into the fried bread in the center. My stomach did cartwheels. "I may not be able to eat all this," I said. "I'm really quite full."

"Eat up now. Eat up or the beggars will take it," she said. I remembered her coaxings from childhood when I would wander across to her kitchen, complaining of how my dinner at home had been too smelly to touch. I laughed at her mimicry.

"Leave him alone," Paddy interrupted. "He's had his fill elsewhere tonight. They have fine cuts of meat down at Deegan's, we hear. And better galavantings for the night of a funeral, too." But Mrs. Quinn was out of earshot. I pretended not to have heard. Commotion was all we needed. I let it rest. Those about, hanging on every word, would notice. Paddy was drowning himself. And at wakes the unpredictable was predictable to those who knew the ritual. I began to pick at the oily food. There was no salt. I looked across at the small dining table. A cellar and spoons were laid in the far corner. I looked about for something to hold my plate. Paddy noticed. "What is it?" he said.

"Salt."

"Stay where you are. I'll get it." His voice was gruff but no longer spiteful. When he reached his chair again, he handed me the cellar, then steadied my plate as I shook the heavy white grains across the black food.

"Too much of that stuff is bad for the heart. From what I hear, you don't have the best one neither," he grumbled.

"It's strong. But the job brings hypertension. Mama exaggerates."

"You'd better watch it. No laughing matter, being crippled in a strange country. I know that if anyone does."

"The university covers all expenses. We're well protected, if not always well paid."

"All covered, eh? Make sure it's not with six feet of earth."

"Jesus, Paddy, you're in a dancing mood tonight. Goddamn, if you . . ."

"I'm sorry. I had the Da on my mind. It was his old ticker that got him, in the end. Mama says that the doctor recommended a special diet, but shit, he plastered everything with salt and ate pigs' toes and backbones until they came out his arse."

"It wasn't that. It was the drenchings and soakings he got on the river, years ago. The spitting out of blood after rowing down from Plassey Falls and the Tail Race. Trying to be a man. Getting the sand in before all the others. Little kids, killing themselves to show off."

"I don't know about that, Thady. I worked with the sand-cotters. It did me no harm. Sure, the competition was there, but it made for more sand and more food on the table. If anything, it was just a little wear and tear on the skin."

"That's how you see it."

"Don't you have to admit that there was a special jumping

in your heart when you carted more than the usual amount of sand uptown to sell on those Saturdays or summer holidays?"

"That is not . . ."

"Eat up that food or you'll have a plateful of grease on your hands. Can I get you another stout?"

"All right."

Neighbors were gathering about the fire. The escaping gush of air rising from the iron-lunged kegs of beer. No more the red barrels, for fear of rats getting through the wood and gorging themselves into madness.

I tasted the first pudgy slice of pudding. The revulsion of flies and gray bacteria-filled storehouses filled my mind. Butchers sluicing the blood from the necks of pigs. Men with wet lips blowing up the skins, ready to fill them with blood, like long over-sized condoms. But having restrained my imagination into sobriety, the pudding tasted rich, like wine that oozes from feet-trampled grapes. I ate ravenously. However, my appetite lost ground at the packet. I had never liked it, even as a boy. Some things had their limit. Packet had its. Grease and milk. Not a delightful mixture. I left it to the side of the plate. Finished, I folded the linen cloth and put it and the plate on the mantel. There was loose change lying near the china dogs. The old memories and urges. New pennies. New notes. But still the old world with all its trappings.

Paddy was back with the pints. Mine had a fine creamy froth. Good stout. It meant a lot at a wake; otherwise you were disgraced all over the parish. I put the glass to my lips.

"Himself wouldn't half mind sitting down here with us, I can tell you, God rest him. Did you hear how he went?"

"In his sleep."

"Right. Who told you?"

"The girl at Deegan's."

"I see."

"By the way, where are Sadie and Maud?"

"Down at Thomond's, preparing the body."

The thought disturbed me. How could they do it? The white stiffening flesh. The matted hair. The limp thing hanging there, already blackening. The eyes staring out into its transfixed memories for all time. The women doing that sort of thing for centuries. They would say how white the body was— like a child's. Some women making a profession of it, just as a midwife might. Good God Almighty! And I even refusing to come near the delivery room when Jennifer had Bernie. As my proud friends had done. Fuck that shit, I said. I don't want to sit around and watch some bloody crinkly thing come out of that part of you I enjoy. It would put me off it for a lifetime. Jennifer had gone into hysterics. Said that I wanted her and the child to die. The parents were called. And I spent the night at a motel, just to get the bloody hell out of there. Women!

Some of Paddy's in-laws entered the room. He excused himself for a minute to greet them and set up the pints. He'd be back as soon as he could, he said. There was more to talk about. I looked at the relatives. Small, mean-looking people. They made no sign of recognition. It had been many years. Paddy married to their half-whore Gertie. Lads used to say that she had ready obscenities on her lips before she began to do a line with my fool brother. And Paddy! Jesus! Casanova of the jetties and green-slimed sandcots. His first bitch. And his last, no doubt. I could not in my reverie, either now or years before, visualize Paddy down among the damp rushes on Cleeve's Bank, hidden from the strollers above and the erect oarsmen on the darkening Shannon, whispering to a cheap classless slut of hopes and promises and dreams. His brown nicotine fingers up her dress. The oily food inside me turned. He had met Gertie at a dance in John Street, a place that the twilight insignificant roamers of the streets frequented. She had worked at the boot factory, the smell of leather always about her. I could smell her even now—the exact aroma. I could place her in a hundred women.

My mother had never liked Gertie. Had even made some

caustic remarks once. Said that it was a disgrace to the neighbors to be carrying on below the lane's light. Courting, giggling, mumbling like people half out of their minds. And till all hours of the night and morning. The girl must have a streak of tinker or knacker in her, she said. Paddy had become furious. A month later they were married in their crumpled just-out-of-pawn clothes. Their cigarettes lit on the very doorstep of the church. Sacrilege? And now the very bastions of Catholicism.

I remembered my own marriage. Jennifer and I had been happy in those early college years before the unexpected arrival of the child and the terrible pressure to make ends meet, finish school, and hold down two jobs. And later, after the breakup, when friends came one at a time and accused her, each in his own words, I felt a genuine sadness. If only it could have been determined beforehand and the entire compass of our lives adjusted. But it was as it was. No avoidance. No excuses but to face the facts. Jennifer had been unfaithful. Other friends had surmounted such obstacles to permanency. Even said that the infidelity actually increased their savoring of married life. Saying, when the wife sins, you know, Thady, the husband is never totally innocent. You're working too hard. You've neglected her. She's been lonely. The world doesn't come out of books alone. You have to make time for other people. Especially your own wife! Give it another try. Give her another chance. I could not see it their way. I remembered the rules too well. Laws engendered from childhood. The voices of the moral and upright women I had known. *When a woman carries another man's gruel in her womb, she is no longer a wife but low filth.* Had there been a shred of choice, I would have stayed. But it was decided. Carrying down the linen, the books, the gifts of Irish crystal, knotted me and drew me up like a hunchback. A man in the hallway asked if I was sick and needed a doctor. But I said no, it was just cramps. Each load took its toll. The night spent retching over the commode at the Cactus Motel. The bile anxious to oust itself from my stomach.

Three months after the divorce, Jennifer was married again. Happily this time, it was rumored, to a simple uncomplicated slob. More like a neighborly teddy bear. I had met him at a Christmas party the year before, but had not at the time suspected his intentions. Or Jennifer's. I did not begrudge her. But I missed the child. The faces. The antics. The touch of another body that was part of myself. I was free except for his support. I would never let that pass, though the spaces between visits sets my name more unfamiliarly on his child's lips.

Paddy was back. "Where were we at?"

"Washing the body. The second baptism. Helping our father into Paradise—which is more help than I ever received from this family."

"What's all that supposed to mean?"

"Whatever it seems to mean."

"Thady, you galling fucker, you mean me, don't you?"

"Not particularly."

"Oh, yes. I know all about how Christy Flannery from the Island Road was the one who took you over to England years ago, instead of me. You had a right to be bitter. But I couldn't, Thady; God knows we didn't have our supper. And Gertie out like a balloon."

"You liar. She didn't have the first child until over a year later. Mama wrote. She . . ."

"Listen, Thady," he said. His voice was lower. He moved his face closer to the red bars of the fire. He put one hand to his mouth. "Listen, Thaed, Gertie was up the pole a month before we left here. Why in the name of Christ do you think I got my arse out of here so suddenly? You think I wanted to leave the river? I loved every cove of that dirty channel and still do. But I can't come back. The first time I'd put little Deirdre in school, the word would be all over the place. The family would be disgraced. Jesus, I dread the day that someone from this fucking town comes to Birmingham. The first thing they'd say is, 'God, Gertie, but isn't she a fine little girl for her age?

How old of a child did you say she was again?' They're thundering villains."

"So you've kept the face up?" I felt compassion for him. His profile brought the illusion that he was being devoured by the fire's heat. Sucked dry by its every flame and scorched to a sapless cinder.

"Did anybody know?" I said. "I mean when you left?"

"The Da did."

"What?"

"It was he who gave me the few quid to get married on and some sand money to get to England."

"I don't believe it. The man was incapable of any affection. But then you were always his favorite. He talked to you. That was something for him."

"You had him wrong, Thady."

"Bullshit. He chased me and paid you to get out of here."

"Don't say anything against him, Thady. I'm giving you fair warning. You asked for a lot of what you got. He was no different than other fathers. They belonged to a time."

A silence fell between us. The fire blazed away, caught by a sudden draft from the hallway. I heard someone slam the half door. The latching sound of the big door followed. Paddy's face showed no malice. He had simply taken his dead father's side as I would have done, perhaps, against a stranger. He began to talk again. "Teaching, Thady. That must have its compensations. You're not out there wet and sorry like the rest."

"There's more to life than being just dry, Paddy."

"That's true, I suppose. But one thing—you don't mind I asking?"

"Go ahead."

"How in God's name did you get into this teaching thing? I thought you'd spend your life just writing poetry and nothing else."

"One has to live. But teaching gives me plenty of time to write and keep abreast of all that's going on."

"I thought you'd go for the poetry and nothing else. You were mad after it as a kid. I remember you wrote one on an old lady who died. You picked her name right out of the dead list in the paper."

"That's right. They published it in the *Weekly Call*."

"One thing I couldn't understand, though."

"What?"

"Well, that you could write about that woman and not even know her."

"It's not necessary to know your subject as you know a friend or a neighbor. You can surmise their feelings and hungers."

"That's not true. And that's your problem, Thady. You try to look through everybody's window and think that because you're better than us on the surface, you're better in the total all of it. You're my own brother, flesh and blood, but you're a complete stranger. To me. To Maud. To Kevin. To Sadie . . ."

"I suppose to Mama, too?"

"She thinks she knows you. But you know that's a lie. You write and the world is made rosy or black by every letter. She held your hand all through your childhood; now you lead her about like a blind woman. You lie to yourself."

"Are you implying that . . ."

"You're fucking right I am. Just like that marriage of yours. I don't know what your reasons for getting into it were. God only knows why. But one thing is sure, you got out in a fine fast hurry. One minute you're there and the next you're gone, like the falling of a hatchet."

"You've seen too many pictures."

"Ha! I've seen *through* the pictures. The pictures you try to create. For Mama, especially. She sits around worrying about you. And Jennifer—that poor girl is thought of as a slut and a trollop. And she only human, like everyone else that's deserted and neglected."

"You know it all?"

"What's to know? We're all human. Jesus, the way you act, you could be a priest of the Inquisition."

"My wife was a whore."

"But it took you a long time to discover that. That's not like you, Thady Quinlan. You miss nothing. You have always had an eye like a leopard. And you damn well know it."

"I was busting my ass every day at the university. I never suspected . . ."

"Or wanted to suspect, in case it cut off your ticket to glory. Bursting your arse for her? Or was it for yourself?"

"I didn't need her support. I had my G. I. Bill and I held down two jobs."

"You never needed anybody to . . ."

"You son of a bitch! You're just like the dead bastard down in . . ."

The fist that smashed into my face obscured in pain and the hot salt of blood the vision of the room swirling in descending spirals until it became a blackness. My mouth, raw and torn, found the granular coarseness of the floor drag against it. I spat and spat but my face was ripped into the darkness, unable to divert itself. My arms were being pulled. Faces over the half door. Paddy standing above me, holding a bleeding knuckle. He had it coming, I heard a voice say. Served him right. I felt a cold damp cloth on my face. My mother was bathing my wound with a soft rag, the whiteness of the material gradually turning red with each touch. *Easy now, Thady. Don't give them anything to talk about. Up on your feet. I'll make the bed for you inside.* I raised myself slowly and leaned against her. I saw Paddy again. He was trying to say something, but the words made no sound.

My room was arranged in the same order as long ago when as a boy I had been allowed to keep its small cubicle of darkness to myself. The secrets, the places under the boards, the unseen corners behind the rafters. The walls were freshly painted. The bed at exactly the same angle. My mother hung my clothes in

44

the closet and, having tightened the blankets warmly about me, said that I should get some rest. A little sleep would do me good. I should never have had the drink without sleep.

Lying there in the darkness, I pondered my reasons for staying far from this place where fish brim the rivers, watched by birds that sing long into the night. Easy late nights on old limestone roads after the dances. With curses and salt under a still bright sky. The whole land equal in its mass to the simple mass of this room. Like the holy picture on the wall and the candlelighting on the table—full of delusions and falsehoods but a veritable sanctum where all the fairy tales, for their absurdity and oddness, really seemed to come true. I drifted into sleep, feeling what the first day home brings to those who know that the last day is immediately being measured in the mind's time by all around. Including your own.

My dreams were terrifying. I dreamt over and over again of water. A circling, suffocating body of water, isolating me from a brightness I tried in vain to reach. My father roared at me. Admonitions, curses, encouragements, sneers. I awoke out of one of these nightmares, the sweat on my face sticking and drying instantly in the heat of the fire, now blazing in the room grate. I'd have to get out of here quickly, before I became a madman like Joe Mulanney, taking revenge on his credit union. My retaliation was not so simple. The first root of all my pain was just blocks away in a cement tomb. All this could not pass without confrontation. My body froze at the thoughts of seeing him. But it was the only cure. It had to be done.

The house was empty except for an old crone who dozed against the fireplace. She said that they had all gone to the deadhouse over an hour ago, but should be back any minute. I dressed quickly. There was hot water in the sink. It soothed the spreading tautness of my face. Some black, dried blood mixed into the water. It floated, then dissolved. My head still swam from the blow and the stale drink. I reeled for a moment but caught myself. The old woman looked at me through bleary eyes as I doused my face in cologne. Her nostrils catching the sweetness. But above it I caught her aroma of Guinness, snuff, clamminess, often sensed on close days in the marble churches uptown. I nodded, but she just stared. Approving? Disapproving? I slammed the half door after me.

5

Paddy

THE OLD SISTER showed us the way back from the deadhouse.
I held my mother tightly. She cried as we walked across the
hospital yard and into the main lobby. The sight of my father's
corpse had begun again the long keening of the women, though
Maud and Sadie seemed to be in control now. My father's body
had not seemed discolored in any way. They had set him there
as if he were sleeping, but of course that is the new way—all
made-up as if just asleep. To me it is wrong. It isn't fair to fool
those left alive. I think it makes their sorrow greater to know
that the person is dead but still looks as if he were dozing. But
the old way was painful, too. I remembered corpses whose faces
were twisted in contortions of agony and pain. Perhaps the ideal

thing would be never to see the body again after the moment of death. That would save a lot of tears. But who would listen to such reason?

The body had been dressed in friars' robes. I had difficulty imagining an old fireball like the Da in such saintly clothes. He reminded me of some tough character awkwardly playing the role of a priest in a picture whose name I could not recall. The Da would have gotten a kick out of that estimation, I thought. I had looked long into his closed face and remembered all the old days and nights and songs and fights. He had been a man's man and only a man could understand his ways. I measured, there at the coffin, the total of his outbursts and tempers, and I found them so far back in childhood and growing up as to be merely old tales spun out of yarn and exaggeration. For all his faults he was my father, I told myself. And I could not have chosen another, since there were no others around to outdo his nature. I had known him occasionally as a man in those infrequent trips back from England with Gertie and the children. He was no longer fierce to me then, but just another tweed-capped man, managing out his days, wishing for better times and keeping the long eye on death. At the coffin, I had thought, he gave me life. I am happy. And for that I am grateful. That is all. Could I ask for any more?

As we passed Baal's Bridge, my mother turned to the girls. "You run on ahead," she said, "and put on the kettle. I'm famished for a cup of tea. And don't wake Thady if he's asleep."

The mention of my brother's name brought back memories of the earlier argument. I had to admit that I had a part in taunting him on. But, somehow, I felt right in belting him. The dead are the dead and by that very fact alone demand respect. Whatever justice there is has nothing to do with those who are left. It's up to God to make the judgments, not a cocky overeducated prick like Thady. My God, he walked in the door of the house after ten years away and had the gall to stand there in front of everyone and call my father a bastard. As if telling the world he hated his father solved anything. A few moments after it happened I regretted hitting him. It seemed as if I too became part of the disrespect. But there was more to my reaction than just a halting of his tongue, I'll admit. I was jealous of him in a way, and wanted to pay him back for all his success and achievement. You get that way, I suppose, when you hear every week how Thady did this and Thady did that. If the Da wronged him, I thought, he certainly was never the worse for it. In my own case, if it wasn't for Gertie and the children, there wouldn't be very much to life. From grueling Monday to horrible Friday, as they say. Certainly, Thady had his sorrows. He may even have been right about his wife. But he was burdened with the weight of nothing but himself. A good life, a car, a prestigious job, tons of money—and still an unbearable son of a bitch. There was no excuse for him that I could see.

When the girls had gone, my mother was silent for a moment. I knew that something was brewing but wasn't sure just how it would come to the top. After a few more steps, she turned to me suddenly and said, "He didn't look too awful black, do you think? Your father, I mean?"

"No, he looked good." I added, "But he's dead, Mama. What difference does it make if he were green or red or purple?"

Her eyes flashed. "You have no respect, Paddy. You showed that this very evening with your brother Thady. You should never have laid a hand on him. All that we have is the family to show to the world, and you went and disgraced it."

"Jesus, Mama, he asked for it. Are you going to . . ."

"It was your place to discourage the bitterness, not lead him on when he got started on the old grudges and spites."

"But Mama, when will you see him for what he is—a self-centered little bastard and . . ."

Her hand shot out of nowhere and slapped me hard across the face. I could feel the cold drizzle cool the burning skin as she stood before me. I felt no anger; only the submission known as a child. I looked into her face.

"How dare you," she said. "How dare you talk to me like that."

"I'm sorry, Mama. They're just words on my tongue. I meant no harm toward you. Honestly, Mama. Listen . . ."

"No, you listen, Paddy Quinlan. You have no right to begrudge anything to your brother Thady. Everything he has he earned. Do you begrudge him his loneliness? Or his hopeless life? Do you think for a minute that I swallow all he says about success and big times? Oh, he has the times and goes the places, but don't you think that deep down he'd change places with you any day? He has neither chick nor child, and when I go who will care a hoot about him?"

"There you go again, standing up for him, like you did against the Da."

"You have a lot to learn, Paddy Quinlan. You grew up on the right side of your father. Thady didn't. And I'm not saying that I'm not to blame for some of it."

"We all got our share of grueling from the Da. Thady was no different. He was no fancy exception. If he'd have gotten off his fat fanny and worked like the rest of us, there'd be no bitterness."

"You never did know your father."

"I knew him well enough to know that he wasn't the demon and scoundrel Thady sees fit to make him out to be. All it would have taken, those years ago, was an apology from Thady, and all would have been well. But no, he was too high and proud to admit his guilt. He was a thief and he should have owned up to it."

"Are you finished?"

"I am."

"Now listen to me. Thady was born into the good times when your father was in England and the money was plentiful. It was I who brought your father home from there, saying that it was no way to keep a family, with him in a lodging house and me with a young child here in Ireland. God forgive me that I should ever have done it. At first he was all right while the few pounds lasted, but then he got in with the river crowd, and every Tom, Dick, and Harry hanging out of him. There wasn't a night of the week when he wasn't drunk and cursing. Oh, he changed, to be sure, but that was later. During those times the only one I had was Thady, and I kept him close to me like he was a floating wisp of straw in a storm. I was afraid, God forgive me, to even let him near your father, at times."

"What has all that to do with the Thady of today?"

"Everything to do. Your father never took to him as much as to the rest of you. There was always a distance between him and Thady."

"And so Thady takes this and builds it into a case with himself as the wronged one?"

"You're wrong. For all that your father was, God rest him, he was wrong in regards to Thady."

"How do you mean?"

"From the day Thady left this town, he cried out to your father for forgiveness. Do you know that not a Christmas or a birthday went by but that Thady didn't send your father a check or a present or clothes or something? Do you know that he wrote your father over fifty letters, asking to be called his son again? But your Da refused to answer a one of them."

"What?"

"Every time a letter would come, I'd get after your father to answer. But it was useless. I'll have to admit that he might have wanted to forgive, but he never put pen to paper. It might have been that he was ashamed of his poor writing in the light of Thady's education. I don't know. But there you are. I didn't dare tell a soul up to this. Your brother Thady was as kind a child as you ever met in a day's journey. Do you ever remember a day when ye were children that he wouldn't give you the sweet out of his mouth? No, you don't."

I was silent. The effect of her words shook me. But changing the years of bitterness could not come in a moment's insight.

There had to be some coloring of the story by my mother. It was only natural; Thady had always been her favorite. But then again, I had to admit, Thady was always my father's scapegoat, too. It seemed that the Da was never satisfied with Thady's actions. The rest of us would do something and there would be an unmerciful clout on the ear. But then it would be forgotten. With Thady the matter was never let rest. I thought to myself, as we walked under the rain, that perhaps the very belaboring of Thady's faults by my father had impressed itself on our minds as Thady's own weakness and laziness. I had come to regard him, despite his other successes, as one who could do nothing right, but worse still, as one who indulged his failure. I remembered how I had shaken my head to Gertie when I heard of his leaving home. Served him right, I'd said. He was asking for it for a long time. Now my mother's words pried open a small crack in my stubborn memory. I thought of those early childhood Sunday mornings outside Saint Mary's Church. The pennies in our hands. The toffee and sweets in Angela Donaghue's window. I remembered my brother Thady standing there with a paperful of Reeve's sweets, dishing them out one by one to Sadie, Maud, and myself. And in a fleeting wisp of uncertain thought, I seemed to see Thady roll up the old sweet paper and throw it in the shore hole. At my glance, he had immediately begun moving his mouth in the pretense of eating his toffee. But I knew that he had left himself none.

In Athlunkard Street the rain began to ease. I turned to my mother and said, "Was there no way; was there no way at all to let Da know how silly it all was? Was there no way you could have talked to him?"

"He was the man of the house. You know the way it is. I was just his wife. I had no say at all."

"But my God, Mama, the damage done to . . ."

"Let's drop it now. It's all over and done with. Your father is dead, so let him rest in peace."

We passed by a new store window before taking the street

---

toward the lane. It was brightly lit. Sweets, tea, bread, toys, and God-knows-what-else crammed the shelves. I thought of my little Deirdre, how fascinated she would be at such a delightful assortment of bright things. It had only been a day, but I missed her and the other children. There had to be something here, I thought, that would make her eyes light up on my return. Perhaps one of those little Irish colleen dolls. Or one of those little boats. There I went again—boats! What would a little girl do with a boat? I decided on the doll for her. There would be time before the funeral. They opened at eight, the sign read.

6

Thady

ALONG MARY STREET the green gaslights flickered their unnatural glow. Near the Munster Cafe, long closed for business, two soldiers staggered from a hallway, one buttoning the cheap knap of his trousers. He asked me belligerently for a fag, but I kept on walking. He shouted that Yanks were the greatest cowards on earth and a tight lot of scum. His friend, noticing the proximity of the Garda barracks, pleaded with him to let it go. They ambled off under the shadows and into the darkness of a nearby lane.

At Russell's Bandroom a light flickered behind the shutters. Some jackeens playing pool and slugging stout from brown paper bags. My father had been a tin-whistler in their famous band of long ago. I remembered the picture on the mantel. His impeccably brushed uniform braided in embroideries. His stiff helmet perched on the head above the severe moustache. A Prussian of the lanes and byways. And we had stood reverently as he marched like a propped-up child to the artifice of the martial tunes. He'd play and play, then drink till late evening, his voice heavy. Demanding his supper. I had often looked at the late afternoon stains on his fancy uniform. Or watched his red beetle eyes search out displeasure. It was then that I first learned to avoid him.

At the corner of the Abbey, a man was hoisting cigarettes on a gourd to two nurses leaning out of their window. They bickered as to price. The man was saying that the cost of living was going up all the time. "Like a hump on a hunchback," he said, and laughed. The nurses giggled. At the green railings I remembered the *clap, clap* of a stick as I beat it against them long ago on my way back from school. To hit each bar had required a slow determined walk, a delay my father rewarded with the belt when I'd arrive home minutes late. I touched the green chipped paint of the bars now. They felt rough to the skin. They ended abruptly at a cement wall around the corner. Under the trees, I could see the blue light above the entrance to Thomond Hospital. I walked across the small footpath to the river wall. Below, the tide was in that indecisive stage when the water turns in slow frenzy, waiting, as it were, for some word to send it like a roller-coaster car off to its holidays in the sea. I once had wondered if the tide was turned by the eels and bream and perch themselves, moving their slimy bodies against the stagnant mass like oars on gigs that brace against the currents. As the tide moved, these dirty coarse denizens would ride the froth out past Tarbert and Foynes, only to hop the next waters on their way back to the nooks and sludge and spewed entrails of the city. And I had thought, what a life it must be to ride and move incessantly, until gaffed and slit by old men who had stopped by for a few short minutes of fishing, before seeing the fourpenny picture at the Ritz. Only I would have wished to be a springing trout or silver salmon. They were rarely caught because they preferred the fresh swift swirls of the center stream.

The Ritz was gone now. A large lighted sign advertised transistor radios in its place. A Garda walked his bike across Baal's Bridge. He stared menacingly at me. I thought that maybe it would be better to take a cab off somewhere and drink, forgetting all, and allowing it to pass into plastic oblivion. Americans had that way with death. Put on a false front. A little less rouge on the face. Rent a black limousine. Hoist a green tent. Hire the clergy for a short eulogy. And bingo! the world was all renewed again on Monday when you took your place at the desk and ordered coffee with cream and a cake doughnut. Not here. Death meant an agony to be endured without surcease. A punishment for your sins against the deceased. You were goaded by spears of reminiscence until the water came and you could take it no longer. It was not your choice but that of those about you. Death was their property.

I turned and faced into the light breeze that was coming up along George's Quay. The shutters of the pub on the corner showed no light in their cracks. The night's revelry had been put away until tomorrow. I went under the stone arch and up the steps to the hospital.

At the desk the elderly sister seemed reluctant to admit me to the deadhouse. Hadn't the family been in earlier? Why hadn't I come then? I explained that at that time I was en route from the dark fields of Nebraska. She said, is that in Northumberland? I said, no, but at the other side of the moon, where my father had once pronounced America to be. She wasn't amused. She would make this exception. But I wasn't to stay more than ten minutes. The matron would be on her rounds by then.

We walked down the corridor of faded green wallpaper. Old cans that had medicine smells lay outside doors from which occasional laughter rose and fell. We turned into a darker hall-

56

way and I heard a child cry. The stench of sickness and neglect hung like a veil of decay in the heavy air. Faces stared after us as we passed weak invalids on their journeys from lavatory to bed. Or nurses waiting patiently to be released. In a small lighted room, a young girl looked up from a steel desk. The sister instructed her to open the deadhouse. Don't let him stay all night, she said in her curator's voice. Then she strutted down the corridor.

The young nurse led the way across a dilapidated court-yard. As I followed, I noticed that she limped. This seemed strange, as though one expected this profession to be immune to sickness. Perhaps she had been sitting on her leg before I came. She fumbled with the lock for several seconds, saying that it had never wanted to open. I helped hold the chain as she inserted the key at a different angle. With a small jerk the spring released. Once inside, she touched a switch to the left, and a faint neon fluorescence gave shape to the small contents of the room. A table with a cross and a white bowl was set against the far wall. Several roughhewn stands capable of supporting coffins lay piled in the corner. In the center, paralleling one another, were lightly varnished caskets. Small cloths like dish towels covered the heads of each box. She pointed to the one on the extreme left and nodded.

I felt afraid. How many years had it been? Ten. A long silence that hoped for shattering but that would now be rewarded with the longest silence. The towel sagged over the rigid face. I could discern the outline of the features. Hard. Relentless. Doors closed to any feelings that might have gone. Oh, how I cried out to you, Bonsha Quinlan, from dried holes and vomit-filled towns, to hope that in your mind ran shadows of my face. The letters that tried to explain my exit, my suffocation. That said I breathed and was hungry for some nourishment lost to me. And the replies came back signed by my mother. Saying that you said this or that—in their third-person well-intentioned lies. The night I left, my mother and sister on the platform, looking over their shoulders, dreading the sight of you. I dreading too, as the train lumbered across the wet dark fields. Each country station had brought terror as men in tweed caps came through doors or stared into the carriages. Looking like you in their sullenness. And the ferry brought relief until I realized that you, too, knew water and could travel and find me in the soot and grime of my retreat. Not until I sailed out of Southampton on the bannered ship *Elizabeth,* waving at imaginary well-wishers, did I know that I had left you behind on your septic sands. All for disobedience. But hadn't it to be more than that? Wasn't it more than an assertion of my will and a fading of yours? What in you made you usurp that natural weaning? I had known chastisement when you came home from England in those early years, and I was a child used to comfort and my own way. But words had followed words when the pain died. Not silence following silence. You were not always indifferent. There were times, before the bitterness, lying against you in the old bed. The smell of the strong twist tobacco all around you like incense. And the feel of your coarse flesh. And the words you spun, your tongue their mandarin. There was a day too, even before you came back for good and took to the river. I, in my Communion finery. My mother pretending to pick up a package from you at the railway station. A black train hissing on the tracks. Suddenly, out of it you came, scooping us up. Around and around like dancers who are forever twined in friendship. We went across the street. You said that on *this* day I could have as many raspberry cordials as I wished. And I did. And I was sick and you held me over the toilet. Laughing. Maybe it was not the words that went first but their laughter, changing to sullen commands. Isolating my movements from yours. A wall of bitterness rising out of the mind's or will's control, as the fangs of dogs whose violence springs from some primeval well of hate below the depths of their very souls. I, as animal bred out of offal into soft flesh, was afraid even now of this old Stone Age savage, dry-docked by death.

Now the nurse grabbed me by the arm and pulled me back from the head of the coffin. "Oh, God, sir! I don't know what to say. I'm awfully sorry."

"What's the matter with you, woman?"

"Merciful Jesus, I showed you the wrong coffin. Your father is over here. God forgive me."

Jesus, I could have throttled her, but looking into the stupid sow eyes I saw some inefficient child trying to make a living, win a man, and produce more incompetents. Instead, I allowed myself to be led to the correct coffin. She lifted the small cloth.

My father was dressed in the ornate robes of the friars, his hands clasped, clutching mother-of-pearl rosary beads. A hood covered his head, concealing the hair that must have been the same whiteness as the eyebrows and moustache. His face was set as though he were enjoying a small joke and contemplating one better.

In my mind, at first, the room had seemed such a small place to contain my father, but not now. He had been easily laid there, dressed in feminine regalia, his eyes pressed closed without a word. I could have pushed the coffin over and watched him at my feet, turned in whatever position he had fallen. I tried to iron the unfamiliar creases of his face back into some memorable contortion or expression, but they were obstinate to change. Perhaps the eyes, if open, would have lent a bridge to the reservoir of memories brimming in my mind. But I knew the improbability of this. No aspect of his face or posture was familiar to me. The years had twisted him out of recognition. In my mind's eye alone he prevailed as an idea that stormed itself across my consciousness at will, to be resurrected and placed in connection with one living entity thousands of miles away in another country and another time. Now that coefficient was gone. To what purpose, then, my creating him in the eyes of colleagues at tired cocktail parties when the humor ran low, and I saying that once he had knocked me senseless with an oar from the sandcot, if they in their minds could not say that this ogre, this natural fierce primitive, was alive and well? And that in my cultured veins ran his hoary blood. I had praised him too, saying that his voice was big and that rooms came alive to his presence. Women at his beck and call. Old lord of the channels and coves and headraces. Formidable, immovable, everlasting. A mountain never stirred but always that by which I measured my life in goings toward or strayings from. A natural magnet whose polarity was as whimsical as a child's windmill. But now a yellow mound of insensible grizzle and gnarled flesh.

The white lips were pale and glazed as altar marble. A faint odor of decay caught my nostrils, and I remembered that here they have not heard of embalming. He had once told me that our bodies contained two miles of intestines. I had replied, that sure would make a lot of mooring rope, Da. He had laughed, telling the other men of my imagination. Now this Da, this man, this rudder of our days, was left behind amid the rough cement blocks of the deadhouse with a few others of his time and mind.

The nurse led the way across the courtyard. The halls inside were aflurry with the changing shifts. At the desk she handed me a small brown paper sack. The words "Bonsha Quinlan" were printed in biro on the outside. I looked inside. An old nightdress, his tie, and a torn pair of drawers. I held the sack tightly and hurried through the vestibule into the dampness outside, my mouth full of bile.

Up Mary Street. Through Gaol Lane. Past the yellow-ochred condemned ruins. Pools of feet water nestling in little channels and locks. Discarded cigarette packs marked Gold Flake and Woodbine. Across the Abbey of stones and dandelions. Between the hill and the noise of the river.

The house on the corner of Sheep Street had not changed since my days as an altar boy, running to make the quick preparations in the sacristy for early mass. Gray cement-washed. Lace curtains. Green-painted sills. A heavy knocker on dark, varnished wood. I raised it gently and tapped a fine but steady rhythm on the brass plate. The sound echoed in the hall. But no stir anywhere. The window dark, the curtains drawn. I looked across toward Athlunkard Street. An elderly man was walking a small white dog.

I touched the knocker again. Five furious bangs shattering the silence. Nothing. A movement. A light above me. The shifting of a latch. The window creaking up.

"Who in the name of God is that at this hour?" Agnes holding the curtain in front of her.

"Me. Thady Aloysius Quinlan."

"What's the matter? Are you hurt? Were ye in a fight?"

"No. I just came to pay you a visit."

"Thady, do you know what time it is?"

"Can I come in?"

"What?"

"Can I come in your house and tell you things and sing you songs until the dawn comes roaring up the main?"

"Thady, shhh. Be quiet. I'll be right down. Stay there."

The window sliding down. A soft scent of perfume in the air. Through the curtains I could see her body outlined against the light. Even in her formless nightie, her figure worthy of exploration. Lie close against the soft breasts. Cradled against the lips. And other places of delight. A light in the hall. The pad of feet. The latch hesitating, then snapping open. The door creaking back. Agnes, her long hair over her white shoulders. Her face vexed but smiling between.

"Thady Quinlan, I'm going to murder you for doing this to me. Where in God's name have you been at this hour?"

"By sea and by land."

"You were in a fight. There's blood on your face. Did it happen at the house? With your brother Paddy?"

"Yes."

"Ye should be ashamed of yerselves. The very night of the wake. Was there terrible commotion?"

61

"We were discreet."

"Don't joke. It's a bad thing. But that isn't all, is it, Thady?"

"What do you mean?"

"You were somewhere else. Thomond's?"

"How did you guess?"

"I can see it in you. You're not drunk, though you'd like to let on you are."

"Can I come in?"

"It's too late, Thady. You know that. There'll be enough seen and heard as it is without I letting you in on top of it."

"Screw the lot of them."

"I'd like to say that. But I've got to live with them. You'll be off and far away in a week or so."

"I'll take you with me to the pigsties of Nebraska."

"Sure you will. Now be a good boy and go on home. I'll be looking for you tomorrow evening after the funeral. We can talk then."

"I want more than talk tonight."

"I know you do. But it's what's on you that makes you say that. It wouldn't be right."

"I could promise to . . ."

"You know it wouldn't solve anything. There'll be times when we can meet."

"Tomorrow night?"

"God, Thady, it's not as if I were promising you a sweet! I'll tell you what, why don't you go on down to Finn's. He'll fix up a bed for you. Tomorrow you'll have pulled yourself up. You'll be in better sorts then. We can all get together tomorrow night at Deegan's. All right?"

"Good-night."

"Are you angry?"

"No."

The sky was clearing of clouds. The white light making mosques of the old buildings. I walked across the stones and debris of the common. The door behind me hadn't shut. I had waited for the sound. Glancing carefully around, I could see her still in the doorway, her nightie catching the wind. She pressed her hand against her thighs to stop the flurry. Fortunate breeze. She caught my deceit and waved before locking the door. I took the corner to the right. Down the foul-smelling lane toward Finn's. Away from Sheep Street. Far south of Higher Brazil Street.

7

Thady

IT WAS NEAR ONE O'CLOCK when I came into Goat Lane.
Finn's small stucco house was newly whitewashed. The windows showed a faint light. I banged on the door. There was a
heavy rumbling noise. The bolt slammed back. Finn in long
drawers adjusting to the darkness.

"Thaed! Come in. Come in."

"Sorry for waking you."

"No, no. I was up. I had a miserable thirst. How did it go?"

"Not good. Paddy and myself had a go of it, right in front
of everybody."

"Jesus, I can see that by your face. Did you just come
straight from the house?"

"I did." The lie came easily. It was better to say nothing. "Listen. Do you still want to go out for a few?"

"We might have time for a sly one somewhere. But it's awful late. I don't know if we can get in anywhere."

"I need more than a sly one."

"God, Thaed, there's no place. Except . . ."

"Except where?"

"Jesus, we wouldn't want to go there. Not tonight. If we were seen . . ."

"We'll go anywhere anytime. I have no ties. Time is my way and my own."

"But the wake? The family? If it was heard that . . ."

"Fuck the wake and every other one associated with it."

"Jesus!"

"Where's this place at?"

"Storan's, on the docks. The whorehouse. Now do you see what I mean when I say that . . ."

"Let's go. I'm on for anything."

"Just a drink, Thaed. Your mother, Chrissie, would have me . . ."

"Are you coming or not? Or do I go myself?"

"I'll come along. Wait'll I put a pair of trousers on. But Jesus, Thady . . ."

"Hurry! Hurry!"

He reached for the clothing thrown across the cot in the corner. The little room smelled warmly of bacon and black pudding. The table was strewn with remnants of a meal. Fried bread. Rasher rinds. Egg yolk. Finn ran outside. I heard water splashing. He was back in again like a shot. "Jesus, it's freezing," he said as he pulled an old coat onto his shoulders. And out into the night with us.

We crossed King John's Bridge and onto the mall, now emptied of Irish soldiers and their painted whores. Only the huge horse gulls remained above their white-limed river wall. In Bank Place a man was watering a horse near the men's toilets, below the sedate customshouse. He strapped the horse viciously, trying to turn its head away from the muddy water. The animal reared, throwing its mane in defiance. But the man became angrier and prodded it with the spiked end of a stick, his face flushing under the pole lights. His frustration seemed bounded not by the animal's need or his own desire to get away to a wife or pub, but by the animal's gall and arrogance alone. I thought of his wife, if he had one, how she in turn would be similarly flailed if her insolence caused the man an inconvenience. Horses and women. I wondered which came first, if, indeed, they were not equal—at once prized and as quickly rejected.

"How far down the docks is this place?"

"Near Clonas Hill."

"Fine."

"Are you sure you want to go?"

"I am."

At Williams Street corner the late buses were collecting their cargoes of young working girls. *Janesboro. Ballinacurra. Ballynanty.* The sweet smells and unperfected made-up faces searched the waiting clusters of young men for a Tom or a Paddy or a John in his brilliantined tier of hair to take them home. I once walked a girl home to Janesboro. Three nights later, on our way to Sparling's pub for a pint, I met her. She was all dolled up and powdered to the gills, her shy smile reaching out to destroy my resistance. Did you meet Finn Keough today? she said. But I said that I didn't and wished her good-night there on the corner near the blowing newsstand. The lads and I laughed at it all, over our stouts, until Finn showed up cursing and blinding. You dirty bollocks, he said. I told you today that I had made the date for you. And you left the poor misfortune there after she coming all the way down on the bus. How am I ever going to face her? There was no appeasing of him that night. He refused to drink with me. There was a limit, he said.

At the *Republic* offices, Finn pointed. "They still remember you in there, Thaed. Keep your picture in the front window for all to see."

"Go on!"

"No. When Joe McGuire raises one of his friends above the crowd, he doesn't want it forgotten in a hurry. There you are there in the front display, your kisser puckered up like a gen-u-ine professor."

The window sported hounds and hurlers and aldermen. In the middle, the large photograph smiling. My cap and gown resting easily. Saying unabashedly to all that this was success. That distance was distinction and reverence. The caption did not even betray the slightest smirk:

Well-known Limerickman, Thaddeus Quinlan, given professorship at American university.

And in the small but glamorous print Joe had forgotten nothing. My participation in rowing regattas. My honors at the Brothers'. My poetry in the local rags. How easily the words, placed so discreetly, could alter the very truth and numb any question of the reality. But then again, what was the reality? I wasn't the best bloody oarsman, but I had tried. All that's required is the effort. I had taken three honors in my Leaving Certificate. That was honors by any standards. And the poetry? A bit romantic, true, but the images and sounds were there. Joe McGuire was perceptive, if not too prophetic at times. He had included the same details with another headline of a few years earlier:

Well-known Limerickman, Thaddeus Quinlan, marries pretty American girl.

"Joe is a good man, Finn," I said.

"And a fine newspaperman. He knows everything that's going on in the world."

"I'll bet."

At Henry Street, near Saint Enda's College, we had come half-circle and could see the Spanish church. Henry Street ran the gamut of laundries, coal yards, and shops, and broke itself in a treaty of small confectioneries down Sarsfield Street.

"Where the hell are we going?"

"You'll see in a minute."

Finn passed in front of me, made a quick turn, and was gone. In a second, he popped back into the light again, emerging from a small indiscernible laneway.

"Where did that come from?"

"It was always here. But it's only lately that it's been used as a shortcut to the docks. Let's go."

At Davis Street we came into the docks. Black ships and barges, still visible in the half-light, stretching in jagged rows off toward the sea, the water here already giving off a scent of the brine.

Castle Wall was a string of nooks and shadows. As we passed along, I was startled by a girl's voice calling from a small niche in the stones. "Short time. Short time, lads," she whispered, in what was her best seduction.

"How much tonight?" Finn asked.

"Five quid."

"Jesus, will you stop. Is it lined with down it is?"

"All right. Wait'll you see. It's all up like a hump tonight. There's lots of strangers in town."

As we passed a stretch of even cement, Finn turned toward me. "She's probably right, you know," he said.

"I'm not broke. I have more than enough for both of us."

"You're sure you won't hang on until another night?"

"There's no waiting. Are you coming or not?"

"You win, like always."

More figures along the shadow-pocked plaster. Hands

68

reaching out from the darkness, brushing our sleeves. The soft murmuring cadence of prices in quids, and bargains and concessions and often the mention of particular talents to suit the various tastes and punishments. All along, the rise and fall of cheap perfumes. And a whiff here and there of coarse Lifebuoy. Some, no longer young, made little play for price but asked if we had a drink on us.

Storan's pub lay in the center of the old dock wall outside the Limerick Steamship gate. A faint glow came through the small exposed portions of windowpane. The rest was cluttered with cigarette ads and other cardboard signs, the lower section shuttered tightly to block off the Guards' prying curiosity. The stained door swung easily into the unexpected glare of the main bar. Men were crowded against the counter, their arms resting on the rails or encircling the waists of the few girls in sight. I looked at Finn. "This place looks like a bachelors' quarters, not a whorehouse."

"It's early for here. Most of the girls aren't down from the town yet."

We sat in a small snug close against the back wall. A few of the men saluted Finn, joking about the three twenty-five and the nag that won it. Finn made two hands, indicating his winnings. They called him several foul names and said that his hammer was hanging in the right place. The word went around the bar like a victorious chorus. A few of the girls looked in our direction, smiling broadly. Finn whispered, "They think I'm in the quids. What harm, it was only twenty bob I won off the bloody thing. That could hurt bargaining."

"I told you I've got money enough."

"There's no need, Thaed. I don't think I'm on for anything tonight."

"Please yourself."

My eyes were becoming more accustomed to the glare. No red barrels in this establishment. A line of Formica tables along the wall. The floor polished to a high shine. Brass and bright crystal. Not unlike a bar somewhere in the Midwest. But the clientele was different. Black dockers, their eyes shifting in their grime like Al Jolsons. Others covered in Rourke's flour, giving off small spurts of dust with every movement. Other men, surely on the dole, their respectable white collars arched above the shiny cuffs and elbows. And the more well-heeled—topnobbers acting patronizingly, an air of quiet gentility about them. Gracing these small encampments of pleasure. They drank whiskeys to the others' pints. And frequently broke blue bills to pay for the drink.

The girls surprised me. I had imagined them all to be of lower class, but I was wrong. Finn had not been exaggerating when he described the change. Some, of course, wore the garish pink and red dresses, their faces caked in paint and powder, inexpensive perfume reeking even to our seats. They hovered about the dockers and laborers. The other, more erect women, sidled against the arms of the better-dressed men. Their hair was not tousled and unkempt but carefully molded in fashionable styles. Their makeup, at least from our table, was careful and slight. Some wore expensive tweed suits or pale cocktail dresses. They were poised and well aware of their attractiveness. They kept a clear barrier between themselves and their more bizarre associates.

The stained glass door opened suddenly. A girl in her late twenties, dressed in a yellow screed of a dress, came into the light. She looked about her, taking in every assignation and friendship at the bar. She paused for a moment, then looked to the back where we were sitting. Finn waved. She smiled coyly. He whispered, "This is the crack, Thaed. A good flake. Is known to give it on tick, too."

The girl sauntered toward our table. She swung a cheap suede handbag, her hips moving awkwardly in a conscious effort at being sensual. I laughed to myself. The girl was above us now. Finn jumping up to give her a seat.

"What'll you have, Maeve?" he said. "A small stout?"

"A Pim Number One."

"A Pim?"

"Yes. Don't you know what it is?"

"Don't I! All right. What are you having, Thaed?"

"Just a pint of ale."

I noticed how he looked at his change and a few solitary bills before ordering. I stood and leaned toward him. "Here, let me get this. Those bloody Pims cost a fortune."

"I know it. But sit down where you're at. It'll be cheap in the long run. She's a good bit of gatter."

"Listen . . ."

"Sit down, I tell you."

As Finn pushed to pay for the drinks, I sat back down. The girl, Maeve, was lighting a cigarette and watching me across the flames. She shook the match. Her eyes were without emotion. Much like the girls in my classes. Confident. Sure of their ability to seduce or halt or manipulate at will.

Now her voice was coming out of her in slow, bored monotones. "Are you English or a Yank?"

"Neither."

"What then?"

"From here. I was born in the parish."

"You still count yourself as one of them?"

"I've only been gone for ten years. That's not a lifetime."

"For some it's enough. What do you do?"

"I'm a professor at a university. I'm home for . . ."

"Oh, Jesus! A la-di-da. A Mister Professor among women like us. It takes a fucking Yank. You're one, all right."

"Listen, you asked me. I told you. I made no slight about your trade."

"What could you have said? I'm a whore. I came by it honestly. My mother was a whore before me. I've worked dirty towns from Luton to Slough, and all the way back to this den of tight pissholes. Can you say the like, me fine-smelling Yank?"

71

I looked around the bar. The conversation had dropped to a whisper. Some of the men pushed their pints away from the edge of the counter. I saw another spit on his hand and turn to gaze into the wall mirror. The better-dressed ones had a look of quiet amusement, shared by the women.

"So what do you say, Yank? Lost your licker? Want a piece of the gay-box or are you here to watch?" Her eyes followed my quick scanning of the bar. But she'd known, I'd felt, without that reconnaissance, the throb and pander of each mindless temper, sucking in its dark nurture. There was only one way to react. Time and place was of no matter. To be whipped by this cauldron of blighted eggs was the ultimate insult.

"People of your kind should know their place," I said. "You're no longer a guest at our table. Get your diseased heap out of here."

The claws across the drinks. Screaming. A demon. *Bastard! Prick! Whore's gett.* And the mad faces laughing. *Let her be. She'll tear his nibs to shreds.* Drink all over me. My face in rivulets of ale and blood. Her paint smeared with each crack of my fist against. From nowhere, Finn breaking in. Holding us apart. Men dragging her out past the jakes door. Spit and yellow pus on her mouth. Finn splashing cool drink on my face. Burning the poison of the honed dirty nails from its fester and crop.

"I had a feeling she'd do that," Finn said. "I should never have left you. She has a bone on for every foreigner that comes in. But you did a good job on her. Her eye is out like a balloon. She didn't cut you up too bad. You just have a deep scratch under your eye. It won't be too noticeable after you clean up."

I looked to see several of the dirty men approach the table. I sat up, expecting further trouble. But their eyes were soft. One said that I'd better get a little iodine for the scratch. Another offered a glass of whiskey. Four pints appeared from nowhere

---

on the table. We were the attraction of the room. The cut forgotten. Talk of women not knowing their place. But over by the bar the women were tight-lipped. The old grudge cheated of its goal. Thinking of their American sisters whose mouths go uncluttered by a man's fist.

A girl in a light expensive dress rose from her stool and walked across to our table. She stood above us for a moment, staring into my face. Finn nodded respectfully. "Hello, Misa," he said. But she still stood, making no indication that she had heard him. Her eyes were a dark green. Her face beautiful in the style of models seen outside old Celtic castles and ruins. The red shining hair. The perfect teeth when she finally smiled and said, "The great demolition team."

"We try," I said, looking into her face.

"May we join you?"

" 'We'?"

"Yes. Babs Sadlier is at the counter." A brunette at the other end of the room half turned in our direction.

"Sure. The more the merrier."

Misa walked toward her friend. They both talked as Babs gathered her handbag and cigarettes. Finn confided, "Thaed, you don't know what you're letting yourself in for. They are the most expensive bits of game between here and Jerusalem. That's Leinster Hotel stuff. You can't touch that for less than twenty quid."

"Money's no problem."

"Not for you. But this pauper. Here they come, oh, Jesus . . ."

The girls were all smiles. The washed teeth shining in the light. Cologne. Cork-tipped cigarettes. Silver lighters like candles in churched women's hands. The red and brown burnished hair. Jennifer had red hair, too, I remembered with nostalgia.

"Introduce us to your friend, Mr. Keough." Misa making a bright face.

Finn was all business and pride. "This is my oldest friend,

Thaddeus Quinlan. Late of Saint Mary's parish and now a professor at the University of Nebraska, the place . . ."

"I know of Nebraska," Misa said.

"You do?" I cried.

"Yes. Principal industries and products are sugar beets, sorghum, rye, petroleum. State capital is Lincoln."

"Amazing!"

"And Father Flannagan's Boys' Town," Babs piped in. We all laughed.

The salve of friendship and fine risings on cold nights as this. Frost across the fancy drinks. The tinkle of crystal and the cash register's bell. All soothing and alive. Conversation from the moistened lips. Even Finn was at ease, his wild head rearing confidently.

A commotion at the door. Clapping from the bar. Joviality breaking out everywhere. Melodeon music striking up. Dancing black-faced men crowding in. Some of the girls from along the wall now in the light, too. Their eyes awake with laughter.

"What the hell?"

"It's the shift from the lime factory. They're a gas bunch. It's Cross and his stokers." Misa smiled across the magic colors of her drink. "You'll hear him in a minute. He's a man who speaks freely."

The man called Cross was massive in stature. His face bloated, seared only by his large red lips. He danced about the center floor, ripping and tearing at a little concertina. As he paraded about, each table complimented him on his agility. *Keep her up. Fine heart. Mad devil.* In jongleur fashion he became caught up in his own excitement, spreading it into everyone and everything. I found myself beating the glass mug on the table. Finn was waving his hands like a conductor. The girls swaying to the discordant but mad music, and the reedy obscene voice. The words spewing out of his wound of a mouth.

Soon a rumble of dark laughter, not known for what at first. Heads turning, searching out the source. Cross suddenly faced us. His short cement-coated tunic was open, its cowl over his head. Dangling from his crotch was a large leather belt which he waved sensuously at table after table. Girls and men falling back in laughter. As he gyrated, he eased the belt farther from its buckle, giving the impression that his false organ was becoming distended in size. As he moved, he veered in the direction of a back table where a man in a dark suit sat drinking alone, ignoring the churl's antics.

"Oh, Jesus, he's after him again," Finn said.

"After whom?"

"That poor misfortune sitting by himself."

"Who is he?"

"He used to be a monk of some order, but he was thrown out over the bottle. He comes down here all the time."

"Because of the women?"

"No. Just to sit by himself. He's a harmless creature."

Cross had reached the man's table. He circled the bowed figure several times, twirling the leather belt in contortions. I thought of the asses in heat, out by the river, in years gone by. Their long black erections protruding into the warm summer's air. Women shading children's eyes from the deathly horror. Cross now flicked his bullwhip of leather. He cracked it deliciously in the air. The man moved. He turned his chair toward the wall. Still Cross pursued. He placed the thong across the man's neck, down over his chest, then back over his face. The man suddenly pushed the table over and tried to escape his tormentor. Cross held him by the scruff of the neck for what seemed an eternity. Then, as if tired of his mouse of play, he threw him against the wall. The little person scurried toward the door. I imagined his ignominy. I was not sure if there were tears on his face. It was sufficient to observe his external agony. But though I sensed his suffering, I could not help him. There were too many enjoying his helplessness. The house broke up at his exit. Cross passed our table. He winked at me. "Watch that one, Yank," he said, nodding toward Misa. "Her beard reaches all the way to her knees." Misa poked him in the belly. I laughed. He seemed kindhearted now. He moved away, playing the concertina. Others, with piccolos, joined him. There was an odd fiddle, too. Ritualistically, the men and women sidled onto the floor in swaying motions of dance.

Some women gathered around Cross and his musicians. Women like beasts drawn to music. They waved their tiny hands like dolls. I noticed Maeve among them. A small bandage covered her eye. She was close to Cross. She glanced quickly at our table but just as suddenly looked away again. She whispered to Cross. He nodded and laughed.

Soon the music from the jukebox began its enchantment. Old songs of the bogs and meadows. Larks in the clear air. Snowy-breasted pearls of girls. Even some of funerals and death. I shuddered, but the music had its own entanglements that lulled the words and purposes. Misa was smiling. I asked if she'd care to dance. We walked slowly onto the floor. Some of the topnobbers were guiding their women across the wax. They smiled. We were part of their clique. I waved to Finn and Babs to join. Too late I realized. Finn pointed to his crippled foot, making hobbling motions with his hands. We laughed.

Misa's body against mine. Her hair brought back memories of Jennifer. It was her hair that I had noticed the first night we were introduced. And I remembered how she had asked where I was from. And I had said, Ireland, where the sun comes up like green fire. I was different from all the others, she said then. From the boy who wrote illiterate notes from his naval station in California. From her Friday night dancing companions in Hot Springs. From her hometown lovers. And after a brief courtship of jaunts and jingles and jests, we were married. Much against her parents' will. They told her flatly that I was an opportunist, and refused to attend our wedding. But we survived their sneers. We were off to a good start, we thought. A job for her in Colorado. Honorable discharge and the G.I.

Bill for me. Acceptance at the university in Boulder. A place in the sun.

Misa whispered, "Are we going to stay here all night?"

"Where can we go?"

"Here or the Leinster Hotel."

"Here?"

"If you want to. I have a room."

"Shouldn't we wait for another song? It's pleasant here in the warmth and good company."

"We can try playing our own harp, unless it's something you'd rather put off." She smiled coyly. A topnobber at the counter who had previously smiled at Misa was watching us closely now, waiting for an opening. I would have to move if I was to make my determination good. A sudden memory of my father crossed my mind, prompted by the man's smug expression. My father had that look in death. I struggled to put the thought away, as I had often done with impure thoughts as a boy. But it persisted. I looked across at Finn. His face was sad and worn. In the light he reminded me of my father, as he used to sit sodden in his Friday night's drink by the fireplace. A sadness induced by the turning from responsibility and the sting of everyday life. I was alive. I would rob the wasp of its sting and crush it by the very act of my own existence. I said to Misa, "Let's go on up."

We sidestepped through the crowd. Nobody seemed to notice our departure, but I saw the glint of Maeve's eyes as we ascended the staircase. Was it a reflection of the light? A freak flash of the bottle or pewter? I decided that she had not even been looking our way. The music contained the crowd as we touched the floor like fairies.

The staircase led us into a long hallway. It seemed to stretch even farther than I had calculated. We walked past several closed doors. Misa turned her key in a room that had no number. She touched the switch. The light revealed a well-furnished apartment. A settee was against the far wall. A large four-poster bed injected the corner with elegance from another time of grandmothers and skullcaps and chamber pots. The curtains were drawn.

I lay across the bed. The thick lush quilt surrounded me. To sink into sleep. To drift away unmoored by ropes of all the times. Misa was beside me, kissing my cheek. "Would you like to sleep a little?" she whispered.

"No. I'll just lie here for a moment. I like this room."

Misa went toward the small closet off the bedroom. I heard glasses tinkle. She called to me, "Would you like a drink?"

"No," I said, laughing. "I've had too much already. You know the effects."

"Not with *you*, surely." I heard her giggle.

When she came back she was clad in a long opaque nightgown. The design was plain except for the tiny lace frills at the neck and cuffs. She seemed more covered than she had been on the dance floor. The lack of the usual indelicacy aroused me. Her body moved under the silk, her thighs showing against the material, then vanishing as quickly into its shapelessness. She took my corduroy jacket and laid it carefully across the chair. I waved her aside playfully and began to undress myself. Thoughts of my sister Sadie picking up strewn clothing came into my mind, but I managed to quiet them. From the commode by the bed she took a porcelain basin and poured water from a large white jug. To the water she added a pale green liquid from a decanter on her vanity.

She was kneeling at my feet, carefully dashing the sweetly scented liquid upon me, the rivulets falling with small rainlike sounds into the basin. What was it that it reminded me of? *Lavabo.* I twitched nervously. The coldness of the water halted the excitement. Or was it just my imagination? *Lavabo.* The celebrant's immaculate hands stretched out for washing before the touching of his Lord. My sister Sadie's hands. Innocent hands. Washing the body of her father. And like a child caught in sin, I was confounded by the thoughts rising in the briefness of the pause to clutch their way through the breach. *Lavabo.* The purifying scent of the water. The anointing and preparing for burial. I felt terrified. "Let up! Let up!" I cried.

But she persisted with the water.

"Goddamn it, get away!"

She sprang from me, her face twisted in hate. "You madman! Have you lost all your wits?"

"Keep away, please. Just leave me. It's not you. You wouldn't understand. I'll pay you. Don't worry. Just get away."

She left the bed and walked toward the toilet. Her face had a bitter sneer as she looked back. I closed my eyes and tried to change the thoughts pounding within my head. They were foolish childish associations, but I could not break their insistence. They had me in their grip, and I could not twist, through reason, their senseless tapestry of guilt. I would have to get out of here.

After several minutes Misa returned. She was fully dressed. "Gather in your pullets' farts you call balls," she mocked. "Have you no shame?"

I found my clothes. I thought of belting her across the face but decided against it. She moved to the vanity. I dressed quickly and reached for my wallet. I placed a twenty-dollar note on the lace doily beside her fingers. Her face was scorn. I had never seen such a look of disgust.

"Are you out of your mind, Yank?" she scoffed. "You couldn't get a whiff of it for that. You're not leaving here without paying me fifty of those. Are you a tightwad as well as a pig?"

I threw another ten on the vanity and turned toward the door. She was screaming obscenities at the top of her voice as I shut the door behind me. I passed quickly through the corridor, found the staircase, and began to descend into the smoke and lights of the bar. From the corner of my eye I saw Finn. He was motioning toward the street. Babs was no longer in his company but leaning against the counter. She was smiling. The woman next to her I recognized as Maeve. Her eyes were bright. Other mouths and eyes and grins were on me. It was then that I noticed Cross. He was stationed below the staircase banister. I made to pass him, but he stayed me with his arm.

"Get out of my bloody way," I said. He merely guffawed in my face.

At the top of the stairs was Misa. She held my green dollars in her fists. I had little idea of what was to come next. The music stopped. Everybody faced the staircase. Then it began. Her voice was strident. It resounded through the silent room in its tirade of derision.

"Here he is, ladies and gentlemen," Misa said. "Our fine Yank who comes to insult us. Let me tell you about him. Yes, indeed, let me tell you about him." A brief agonizing pause and she continued. "He is smaller than Michael Brady, than Sean Connally, than Phil Quilty, than Peadar Quinn, than Tim Scanlon, than Raef Moloney, than Dick Troy, than Lalla Daly . . ."

Laughter. Pounding for more. Hands waving. Scourging the air. I tore at Cross but he was immovable. Finn rushed to assist me. The men and women were four thick to block him. He fell helplessly against the door.

"Smaller than Con Donaghue, than Taig Quilligan, than Denny Cunningham . . ."

A ritual of torment as old as the green hills and older. No letting up. Names brought various references, and shouts issued to add to the song of spite. Misa stopped without warning. She came down the stairs slowly, her hips moving in seduction. I saw an opening in her hypnotic effect and rushed Cross. But he had anticipated my move. He pinned me firmly. Misa was beside us. She carefully ripped the green bills into shreds, each particle becoming smaller and smaller with every tear. She raised the worthless papers above my head and dropped them all at once.

"Here is your worth, Yank," she jeered. "Small pieces for a small man, smaller even than the bollocks, Lou Curpin."

A great thunder of applause. The end of the pit. Cross turned away. I was immediately ignored. For seconds Finn looked at me there on the worn steps. He was immobile. Then, as if awakening from a dream, he came to my side and led me outside. The air of the river felt good.

"They set you up, Thaed," Finn apologized. "You know that?"

"That's okay," I said. "I got what I came for."

"You did?"

A taxi passed. I shouted. He went by without noticing. Finn and I walked in silence to Thomas Street corner where the new hackney cars were lined up waiting for late customers.

8

Thady

THE HACKNEY DROPPED ME at the head of the laneway. I
walked slowly in the direction of our door. The house seemed
to be in silence. I peered through the keyhole. My mother was
against the hob. Maud stood at the table drying the delft, her
body hunched slightly by the weight of her belly, distended with
child. Sadie dozed in the sugan chair, rocking slightly to and
fro. There was nobody else in the kitchen.

I heard footsteps in the lane. I pushed open the door and
stood in the warmth. Maud stared at me for the briefest instant,
then flung herself at me. "Thady, Thady! Jesus, love, how are
you?"

"Fine. Fine. And yourself? My God, you're as big as a house."

She laughed. "That auld fella of mine never leaves me alone when he comes home from England. But sure God, Thaed, I loves it!"

She held me close against her.

Sadie had awakened. She rushed across the earth floor and put her arms about me. "Oh, you look grand, Thady. Doesn't he?"

"He does indeed," Maud enjoined.

"If he wasn't my own brother, I'd run off with him," Sadie cried.

They had not noticed the new cuts on my face and must have felt it better to ignore the earlier bruises. I was relieved.

My mother looked up from the fire. "If you spend your time romancing, he'll die right there of famish. Wouldn't you ever think of taking his coat and pouring him a cup of tea?"

The girls fussed and made themselves busy about the gas cooker. I went to my mother and kissed her. She was perfectly calm and collected. None of the earlier hysteria showed on her face. Then I remembered that it was she who had put me to bed.

"Are you okay now?" I asked.

"I am, love. It's only when the big crowd gets to talking and bringing things up that I get upset. I'm ashamed of myself for the way that I dragged out of you today. I should have been taking care of you after your long trip instead of giving the job to strangers."

"Will you stop!"

"No. No. You're the man of the house now."

"What do you mean? I'll only be here for a short time. *You're* the important one."

"No. No. You're the master of this house. It'll fall to you. You're the oldest. It's only right. Your father will have passed everything on to you."

"I don't want anything."

"It'll be yours all the same, to do what you want with."

I ate the small brown sausages placed before me. Their spice mingled with the hot tea.

"You didn't see the other fella uptown, did you?" Sadie said as I blew across the tea to cool it.

"Who? Paddy?"

"No. Paddy's in bed. Kevin. He went off in a stupor after we left him at the deadhouse. We haven't seen sign nor light of him since."

"He'll be okay."

"He's probably on the Dock Road drinking with whores and tinkers at this hour." I looked across but there was no malice in her face. She did not know.

"Stop it," my mother shouted. "Stop that talk right now."

I thanked them for supper and said good-night. I was tired after the miles and the long journey.

9

Thady

I AWOKE EARLY, the morning light across my eyes. There was a taste of sourness in my mouth, though not unfavorable to another pint or two if the public houses were open at this ungodly hour. My watch said seven-thirty. Two and a half hours to opening time.

I made my way through the quiet house and into the scullery. Nobody up. Sleeping the sleep of peace. I used to be the first up, too, long years ago when we'd be off to Kilkee or Salthill on the excursion bus from outside the parish gate. Kind ladies taking the tickets. And away with us over the hills and down the belly-sinking back-of-the-bus dales. Some taking pills to keep the stomachs in their skins.

The table laid this morning. A place for all of us. One. Two. Three. Four. Five. Six. Seven. Still counting my father in, and he down the block with the other fellows who could care less about food.

I went out into the backyard and let the cock spurt its icy water over my head, numbing me into shivers. Back inside like a shot. Rough towel. The scrape of the razor across the face. Wash the teeth. A touch of the lotion after the face had time to close its small pricks and wounds. But it burned even after the pause. My suits were pressed. My shoes at a high shine. Clean underwear, if perhaps a little rough from the Persil. Thank God for women, at times like this.

I eased the front door open, careful not to wake the sleeping mourners. The wreath on the knob startled me, its black crepe fluttering in the early chill.

Bernard Mary Quinlan. Died April 1st. Funeral at ten o'clock from Thomond Hospital. On his soul, dear Lord, have mercy. R.I.P.

Bernard Mary. I'd never known. Named after the Virgin like all the others before his time and after. Once I'd asked him his full name, and he'd replied that full is what you are after eating a free turkey.

So ten o'clock was the time. With an hour before that for the public scourging of the family in the deadhouse at Thomond Hospital. And a quarter hour of grace. Fifteen until nine. And it now eight o'clock. Forty-five minutes for a quick jar. Somewhere.

Kelly's pub on the mall was shuttered tight. I tried to peer through the casements, but a dark curtain inside obscured any trace of activity. Around the back the jakes, too, were sealed off. A huge rusty lock keeping the unanointed out until the chrism-hour of ten. I was about to drift off down the mall when I noticed the curtain of the kitchen section flutter and a hand wave through the glass. I edged closer to the pane. A woman's head scanned Keeper Place, then the mall, and was instantly gone. A few moments passed. The door to the living quarters creaked open. The woman in bib coat and fine blond hair was well known to me. Lizzie Kelly.

"Thady Quinlan, come in quick before I lose me license."

I obeyed. The parlor was dark as pitch, the only light coming from the fire in the grate. A cocker spaniel lorded himself by the irons every second or so, getting up and scratching the rug as if arranging some obstinate straw into a more comfortable position.

"Kick him up out of that, and make yourself a seat by the fire. I'll be back in a minute with something for you."

"What's his name?"

"Pudgy. But he answers to Savior. The lads nicknamed him that because he keeps arranging the rug to suit himself. They say he thinks he's in a manger."

The dog sniffed me, then planted his backside across my shoe. Being a momentary lodger myself, I let him lie. It was cozy enough for two of us in the little room. A man could fall asleep again under the darkness and the flying furious flames.

Lizzie was back, holding a small tin tray aloft. A pint of Bass and a water glass of Paddy's. "Here, Thady. This will put a little warmth in you. It will take away the thirst, too. I heard all about ye down at Deegan's last night. Shame on you, Thady."

"We were on our way here when . . ."

"No, thanks. I have enough trouble. Maura and myself had to call Blackie out of bed to clear *this* place."

"Thank you for letting me in. There's no one up at the house yet. I thought I'd forego the eggs and rashers."

"You have nothing in your stomach?"

"This good liquid will be more than enough. How much do I owe you?"

"Will you stop! Drink it up at your ease. You can let

yourself out by the back. Cross over into Troy's yard and up then by Carey's. I've got to make the beds and God-knows-what before we open. I'll be seeing you after. Keep the heart up, Thady. Your mother and all of them will be depending on you."

"I will. And thanks again."

I sat back in the old chair full of buttons and clumps of hidden straw. Probably stuffed by a man named Walsh, who used to take a month to stuff a rag doll. Or Annie Frawley, who'd make a shift for a flea if he'd wait around until he was an elephant. Good old days of plenty of time. *Take your ease. Sure you'll be long enough dead.* The clock on the wall struck the half hour. Must be off. Sorry, doggie. He looked up disgustedly, and settled himself, through his usual ritual, against the fender. Better in the end, I suppose he figured. More predictable.

At Saint Mary's Church a wedding was in progress, nearing its end by the looks of the whites and blacks and blues and shoes and hats coming onto the green lawn. Faces shiny, powdered, adorned. On old hags in threadbare coats or new satin suits. All leering at the pink bride under the arm of a gawk in his dispensary glasses and tails and striped trousers. Agnes's husband had probably been like him on her day of days, before the nights we all know to be the grit of it. And my own wedding, God knows, was not much better. A little more expense. A few extra cashmeres and bouquets and sagging sopranos. The bridal party was now over by the evergreens. Yellow teeth lapping up the early sun and little intimate obscenities. Waiting and promising the impossible. For they had their reasons. And would examine them all the days of their lives. After the wine and free porter had gone through the kidneys and into the sea.

I strode fast as the hands of clocks in huckster shops clicked closer to the hour. Late for his funeral. For all he'd been, I owed him more than that, I thought.

Mary Street was a market of cars and carriages and bicycles. Horses rearing at horns. Men against the walls, sucking on fags. Dung all over the roadway leading to the deadhouse. Black limousines honking at smaller motors, seeking their sexton priority. Women in clusters, all eyes for the mourning carriage. Waiting for the matron of death and her children. Not recognizing me as yet. The safety of faces unfamiliar to me in their grubby stiff collars and shiny lapels. All serene. Like bees preparing for a dance, retelling their honeyed exploits. Car doors slamming. Black scarves for the occasion. Black stockings up to the pink underwear. Hackney drivers with short tempers saying to others of their profession to get that fuckin' Volks out of the way and not be blocking the street. The mourning carriage will be along any minute now and it shouldn't be hindered.

A hand waving from over by an iron gate. Below the blackened windows with women peering through the curtains. Finn Keough dressed in fine topcoat and heavy scarf. Calling to me. I moved through the crowd. Now they were recognizing me. *Sorry for your troubles. God, I'm terribly . . . Is your mama all ri . . . ?* Oh for a word to say to them. There must be a word or a combination of words for occasions such as this, I thought. *I do,* for marriage. *I do renounce,* for baptism. *I reject and condemn,* for conversion. But what for death? No answer. Now only the words about. About this frenzied square where the execution of the living was the prime concern. What to say? A phrase that covers all. All in you. All in them. All to come later. And my mouth was saying it at every turn. It was working. It was making them fall away, satiated, satisfied. Saying, he's the teacher boy. A refined way with words. The outside world makes them that way. Look at the fine cut of him. My mouth enunciating the words. *I know. I know. But these things will happen.* Easily summed up, added, subtracted, divided, squared, and put away.

Finn's big hand holding me tightly about the waist, the other keeping a polite but firm banister between them and me.

"Are you all right, Thaed?"

"I'll be fine. It's the close quarters."

"That's it, here. The suffocation. You're a hard man. You'll make it."

"Thank you."

"Here they come, Thaed. They're in the mourning carriage."

And there it was. Rising through the swell of beetle men and scattering coats and pockets of small color, the black rearing mastiff horses foaming their arrogant way. A man in a high hat whipping, whipping the leather thongs, flagellating the wet, steaming skin along the fine haunches. *Here they come. The mother. The daughters. That's the oldest boy over there with Finn Keough.* Moving in closer to gawk. My mother pale as the doors opened, and Maud and Sadie stepped onto the iron spatula of a step prodding its way out of the side of the carriage. My mother next. Shoes on her feet, of the black she always hated. Holding the staves of beads in her hand. Hastening out of the chanting crowds into the passageway of the deadhouse. Her pitiful fish's face, bloodless and livid, soon disappeared into the black hole, followed by Maud and Sadie, their eyes covered in the thick veils.

"You'd better get over there, Thaed," Finn said. "It's only right."

"Will you come across with me?"

"Sure. Come on."

Through the clutching hands. Finn pushing the reluctant arms and thighs and shoulders to the side. Rough here. Gentle there. *This is family. Out of the way. Please! Get out of the bloody way, for Christ's sake.* Paddy and Kevin making their paths in our direction, too. Paddy stern-faced.

"You left early," he said to me.

"I wanted to be away from the scavengers."

"There were enough of them around the house this morning. You had a drop?"

"Kelly's. Lizzie opened up for me."

"You should have woke me. I'd have gone off with you."

"They needed you, Paddy."

"And not you?"

"You'd better go up there. I'll stand behind. Mama will be all by herself with the girls."

At once the darkness inside was blinding. The eyes eventually making out the long varnished box, laid out alone now in the center of the weeping walls of cement and hurried plaster. All along, in corners and nooks, the relatives settling themselves at vantage points. Mama in the center. Maud to the left. Sadie to the right. Paddy behind Mama. Kevin dangling awkwardly between two strangers. I stood with Finn away from all the activity. Mama glanced behind and caught my eyes, only to look away again at the hooded figure risen out of the varnished coffin. Breaking her gaze to touch a familiar hand or mouth. What in the name of Jesus must have rested in her memory? I asked myself. From a childhood of sour milk and rag dolls, to girlhood and smirks and smiles and a few boys who came to shape and fleeted into the tide. Until *he* came. Loud, proud, and handsome. Handsome, she'd always remembered. She loved that. She, a small plain consumptive girl. Her teeth all wrong. Her hope all right. Towering in he came, in his green cardigan and mad words. His voice like the lark's. A turible of all-devouring sound. Mama's only love. To be granted all. Forgiven all.

Look quick. The girls are keening. Girls misses their fathers.

From the doorway, the shuffle of feet as the approaching priest in surplice and soutane and black stole moved confidently through the awed crowd. *De profundis clamavi ad te Domine: Domine exaudi vocem meam. By reason of Thy law have I waited for Thee, O Lord.* And one night long ago wasn't he supposed to wait for me outside the Ritz Cinema, after I getting the two-pound prize for my essay on the poor children's excursion to Ballybunion? His Lordship, Mayor Collins, presiding. And didn't my father fall asleep as the Irish dancers ceilidhed around, kicking the wind. And didn't he never come out. And I waiting there in the torrents of rain until the walker had to go down and wake him. Out he came and says he, God, son, when they started playing all them lovely songs, didn't I doze off and think I was down in Kilkee on me holidays.

From morning watch even until night, let . . . Dominus quis sustinebit? Now the sprinkling of the water falling on the burning cheeks from the perforated gong. Only it struck no sound. Merely cooled where it fell. *Exorcizo te creatura aquae in nomine Dei Patris.* The candles about the coffin spluttered their light, faltering, then soaring to brightness again. My father basked in the moving brightness.

The sound of the celebrant's reedy voice rising and falling like the canvas of old ships whose sailors have gone inland. Beating. *Mea culpa.* Beating. *Mea culpa. Mea maxima culpa.*

A commotion in the corner. Two men in dark suits held a huge varnished cover between them. As they approached the coffin the priest's words grew more delicious on his lips. Sucking, savoring, spitting out the syllables that had no connections in his brain. I heard the women behind me whisper, and the word circled the room, hushing the dissonance for a moment. *It's time. The oldest brother will be first to say good-bye.* Nudges pushing me forward toward the coffin, but I held back. Still, I was moved closer by the sheer power of the shoulders and thighs and arms, until I was level with Paddy. He looked at me crossly. Are you going to say it? he said. I shook my head. The pushing stopped. No touch, no urging, no persuasion. I wanted to tell him why, but he wouldn't have understood. Before I could settle it more, Paddy swung forward into the crowd, reaching the open coffin in strides. He stood poised above it for a second, then, leaning on the silver handles, he bent forward and kissed his father. His prolongation of the kiss was met by small prattles of comment about, but they were stifled as he rose out of the coffin, his body shivering in a tremor of pain. I wanted

92

to say, Jesus, Paddy, don't take it so hard. *These things will* . . . Oh, my God!

Paddy bowed back to make way for Kevin. The boy angled through the crowd. Reaching the bier, he made a perfunctory touch of his father's hands and stared unbelievingly into the face. When he turned, his eyes were drenched in tears. *These things will* . . . But no, that was not enough. The words were not enough. There was something more. Something to be thrown up and out. There must be. Something to neutralize— an antidote as water is to fire, as soda is to acid, as chrism is to sin.

My sisters cupped about my mother, leading her forward. She moved, her body convulsed in agony. Together the three women lay across the coffin, keening with the torrents of anguish rising up out of them as sweat rises on stabled animals when the frost strikes their warm bodies. Men at the other side of the room pressed obligingly against the box to steady it for this, the women's last farewell. *Farewell.* But the word means "May your destiny be good." Not even pertinent here. But why then the word, for Jesus' sake? A word that means nothing in a situation that should have a corresponding word to alter or soothe or splice or salve?

The women's screams were broken now, and my mother's voice gave way like that of all the women and mothers before her. *O Jesus, Bonsha, love, what in Mary's name am I going to do without you?* Women from all around centering toward her, consoling, cajoling, touching, squeezing her into them. A mass of females, pressed on by their own identification with sorrow after sorrow, and by their men who had known sorrow, too, but had left it to the women to say it for them. Because it was their way. As it was their way to give the life in the womb and then retreat into the shadows as they were doing now, frightened and full of pity but incapable of its expression. Paddy and Kevin moving to the side of my mother and the girls. And I back there, separate in my expensive cloth and white linen. A sepulchre within a sepulchre. Watching.

The strange men in black measuring the cover for sealing. Undertaker's lackeys. Spinning the butterfly nuts. Whirling off the empty bolts. *Do you have her, Willie? They're all off on this side.* And in me a welling up. Strangers regarding him as a chore and nuisance. Spinning their frigging butterfly nuts. Over his hard, crusted forehead, now dying beyond the first death. Old head. Longed to touch all these years. *Damn! Damn! Damn all of you! Out of my way! Get out!*

The people almost expecting my bursting forward. Moving like ruddered water at my lunges. Only the strangers with their nuts and bolts aghast. Reaching the cheap box. Looking into the closed eyes below me. In the square of colored light. I leaned forward. My hand clutching the stickiness of the varnished wood, gluing me to it. The pulse quickening at the sight of the shut face below me. The barricaded door of mouth, once capable of spit and early morning poison. You bloody blackguard, he'd shouted, slipping behind me that day long ago, his eyes like coals. My legs outskirting his age and flailing talons. He had caught me in the small act of deceit. *Jesus, Da, it was only a pound I took, for Christ's sake.* A shilling or a pound, he'd roared, you're a liar. Every week you held back on the sand money. Not man enough to ask for your due. Stealing the family's food. A dirty little thief. Down the lane we'd ran with women and children gawking out over half doors at us. Two madmen crucifying one another with fists and words. Some were laughing, knowing the routine. Their own blood no different. Even egging him on. When I outdistanced him, his voice was resonant and threatening. *Never darken my doorstep again. Do you hear? Do you hear? Do you hear?* I heard. I had a few pounds in a post office book. A willing friend in Luton, Bedfordshire, who'd put me up anytime, he'd said, and get me a job on the buses. I looked into my father's face, all puffed and panting that day. *Damn you! You mangy old bollocks. Go back to your filth and drudgery. I'm free of you.* I remembered how small he'd looked back there in the lane, hobbling after me. *Never darken my doorstep.* The words hanging in my soul all these years.

Had my deceit been so great? A pound could only buy the pleasures of one small Friday night in which to hide away from the sleet and cold in the back of a rancid picture house. Had I deserved this public ignominy there in front of the scoffers whose children were ignorant like them, but who found delight in my humiliation? And what of his words? *Never darken.* I remembered their sting in my mind that morning under the drizzle. And how I had clung to them over the years, drawing myself away from him inch by inch, in my contemplation. And *my* words. *Mangy bollocks.* Torn up from out of me through desperation. Why? I asked myself. Why his hate and my scorn? There was something deeper than both of us. Here at the cycle's center I felt its presence as real as the clammy bodies about me. But where were the words to set the judgments? I tried in my mind to weave the answers, but they eluded me. There was no focusing of my feelings, no charting of my thoughts. I knew there and then that I had lost. Words between us were dead. He could not defend himself. I could not condemn and be sure. I had known him in good and bad times. That the good were first and the bad last bore no consequence. Time was eternal and without order. Just a sickening, lingering present with me breathing heavily at the center. It was now or forever. I would not turn ever again. And I knew I would care and not care until my own death. I bent across the still cadaver. My lips found its lips, and I kissed, burying my flesh on the hard grizzle, cold as old and wintered machinery. *Farewell. Farewell.*

I wiped tears from my face and stepped back. Paddy touched my shoulder, moving me into the small circle of the family. My mother rested her body against my arm. The men were waiting for the command to lower the small perforations onto the waiting bolts. I nodded. A quick settling of the holes.

95

The spinning of the butterfly nuts. The final sprinkle of water and the priest's *Requiem aeternam*.

We raised the sealed casket onto our shoulders. I took the head. Paddy and Kevin were behind with Finn. As we moved through the crowded deadhouse, hands shot out to touch the rough wood on our shoulders. Men on every side using their palms in an upward bracing, making the weight as inoppressive as possible. The coffin seemed not to be on our shoulders at all but moving in a current of buffeting hands, drifting effortlessly toward the glass and chromed case of the waiting hearse. There was a momentary heaviness as the wood clamored against the slides, but it was gone as the coffin hit the oiled rollers and rumbled into the shiny encasement. The black beetle undertaker closed the glass behind it.

10

Agnes

BRIDIE AND I were standing against the Munster's window when they carried Mr. Quinlan's coffin out of Thomond's dead-house. The two brothers and Finn Keough, with Thady at the head. I looked closely at him. His eyes were sunken in his head as if he had been crying. There was no more of the wildness of last night left. I wanted to go to him and say that I was sorry for being a great big snob the evening before, worrying about my neighbors and their dirty little thoughts and words. I wanted to say that he could come any time, any place and that my door would be open. I needed his company more than he did mine. What kind of woman would I be, I asked myself, if I couldn't console and warm a man in his distress? A barren tomb of a woman who never had a child in her womb, but who could nurse those who were hurt as much as the next one. Wasn't that why we were made? I thought to myself. But it was too late now. I had let the opportunity pass.

Bridie nudged me. "Why don't you go over and offer your condolences. There's your chance to be near him again."

"Bridie! How can you say such a thing the morning of his father's funeral? Look at his face. At the pain."

"Well, I'm just telling you. Tomorrow or the day after he'll be wrawked up by some smart dolly uptown. Or he'll be back to his fine women in the States. Don't think that he doesn't have his share after him."

"Bridie, stop it right now. I won't have that sort of talk. I spoke to the man for a few seconds last night, and you have me in a swoon after him. There's nothing at all between us. I wish you'd grow up."

"Oh, la-di-da! No mention at all about he coming by your place in the middle of the night and shouting up at your window."

"Who told you that?"

"Walls have ears and eyes."

And there it was out in the open, as it always was. I could hear the gossip. *She's mad after him. He's crazy out about her. It was love at first sight.* And there would be no sparing of the scandal, either, on more bitter and lonely tongues. *Imagine, the night before his father's funeral. The cheek of her, and her poor husband away in England. And Thady Quinlan's wife back home in America waiting for him.* And it would all go on until it tired itself out, and they found someone or something else to latch on to. That was the way it was here. And it was easy to see why. When life has no romance, and there are no great mountains to climb, and when one is beautiful for only a few short years before the crows'-feet tear the face apart, what else is there? Exaggeration and gossip. I could see that, but I had no right to criticize. I was as much part of the daydreaming as anyone else. To think that Thady Quinlan would give me a second look! I had to be childish and simple in the mind. I really had. Bridie wasn't all wrong. The minute he stopped off uptown at the Regency or Dunmartin or the Leinster Hotel, he'd be wrawked up like a silver thread. And why wouldn't he be? The cheek of me. If one of his friends from the States saw me, I'd be a holy show. But I couldn't help myself. I kept welcoming in the daydreams like a child outside Fleet's window at Christmas. God find pity for me!

The hearse pulled out from the curb. I saw Thady talk to the young lad beside him. Their heads were going up and down. I felt relieved that he had someone to keep his attention. I knew what it was to ponder sorrow, and I wouldn't have wished it on anyone.

At Baal's Bridge the cortege angled slightly, and Thady's face was turned for a moment in our direction. Bridie waved her hand. I turned on her suddenly and grasped her arm. "That's enough of the play acting, Bridie," I said. "That's enough."

She gave no argument but simply drew her coat about her. Thady had not seen either of us. I thanked heaven for that.

We walked briskly down the mall. I had wanted to see the coffin to the grave, but there was too much to be done at work and no help other than Bridie. If I rushed, I could have the floor swept and new sawdust laid before the evening crowd began to traipse in. And the glasses! The mountains of glasses to be done!

"When we get back," I said to Bridie, "if you'll get on the mirrors, I'll take care of the glasses and the floor right away. That way we'll have a nice long break before we open up again in the afternoon."

"That'll be grand," she said. "And we'll have a little chat, then."

"Fine," I replied, seeing as plain as day her intentions but not being able to change the course of things.

11

Thady

THE MOURNERS RUSHED toward cars and carriages. Paddy and I saw my mother and sisters to the mourning coach and returned to take our places behind the hearse with Kevin and a few old stooped bandsmen. There was a young boy, too. I recognized him as Gerard, Maud's oldest child. He nodded to me as we took up our lines of importance.

"Can I stand with you in the first row behind Grandpa Bon, Uncle Thady?" he asked.

I said, "Sure, Ger."

The procession moved out slowly. As we reached the center of the street, the hearse picked up speed. I looked about to see the reason for the sudden hurry. Another hearse was approaching from the west. Perhaps to cart away the man I had mistaken for my father the evening before. They were clearing them out fast.

Over Baal's Bridge. Down onto the flat road and up through Irishtown. At Mungret Lane a carload of tinkers pulled against the curb to let us pass. Wild faces scarred from a hundred bottles, knives, and infectious dirt. An old man among them doffed his hat in respect. The younger redheaded scions followed suit. One crossed himself. Another fidgeted with the long whip in his fist. After we had passed, they screamed an obscenity at their horse and were gone in a wild canter down the street. The boy, Gerard, noticed my interest in them. "Padraic Colum wrote a poem about wild men like that," he said.

"You mean 'A Drover'?"

"Yes, Uncle Thady. And the other one. What is it?"

" 'The Old Woman of the Roads.' "

"I know that by heart."

"By heart?"

"Yes."

"That makes two of us then."

We were coming out of John Street and into the square below the Cathedral of Saint John the Companion. Passersby searching our faces for the proper gradation of bereavement. Under the sky of light but no shadows. The men, hands behind their backs, starting up lively conversations. Frowning, nodding, saying that it was good weather for this time of year. Or how a friend was shifted only the night before and he not next nor near the fifty mark, the poor misfortunate man. Little bonnamb-faced women on the paths eyeing us closely.

To my left Paddy was giving advice to Kevin. *Try to stay on the job. Get a bit of money together before you take off. Any chance of you picking up a trade?* Something about me. How I probably could get a job anywhere. Even here. To be considered, maybe, I thought. Behind me, two relatives were on the subject of cancer and how one had seen an actual lung on display right in a window uptown. Like a fuckin' kipper it was, he said. Ah, but Jasus, said the other, dead with fags and dead without them. Beside me young Gerard walking erect. Almost my own height. Only a small snotty child when I'd left. Grown into fine scholarship, they had told me. Two secondary grants. He was ripe for conversation.

"How's school these days, Ger," I opened.

"Oh, fine, Uncle Thady," he said.

"Do the masters still beat it in?"

"Just sometimes. They've gone from that."

"I see."

"What do you teach, Uncle Thady? Grammar? Composition?"

"At first I did, yes. Not now. Literature mainly. Late eighteenth, early nineteenth century."

"But do you cover Irish writers or do you just consider the British?"

"Of course. Without Irish writers where would English literature be?" I smiled. He looked pleased.

"We're on Yeats now," he said. "Are you familiar with many of his poems?"

" 'The Lake Isle of Innisfree' and 'The Wild Swans at Coole,' by heart."

" 'Sailing to Byzantium'?"

"Surely you're not learning that? We never went further than 'The Stolen Child' in my day."

"We are. The master taught for awhile near Sligo. He thinks that W. B. Yeats is the greatest poet after Shakespeare."

"I won't deny that."

"He made us learn 'Sailing to Byzantium' and 'Among School Children' by heart."

"What was his interpretation of the first one? A crying out to return to a pure state of Art?"

"No. He says that most people are deceived by the poet's technique in the poem. That he was, in fact, not advocating that at all."

"What then?"

"It's his opinion that Yeats is not the narrator of the poem."

"He's using a persona?"

"Yes. That's it."

"Go on."

"He says that the overpowering images of nature confound, by their sheer force, the surface argument for Art alone."

"He does now. That's interesting. We'll have to explore some of those 'salmon-crowded' seas at a later time."

" 'Mackerel-crowded,' Uncle Thady."

"Ah, yes, of course."

This master. Some village peasant spreading a new-churned gospel when the poet is safely stored away under his promontories. I had once picked some pebbles from the grave near the Rosses. Lived near Sligo, this master, did he? Studied down by the hearth, and by that alone linked himself with the ever-fleeting spirit of the bard. I'd like to meet this caperer, I thought. Brilliantined head. Cheap tweeds. Honors Leaving Certificate. Big man on the Galway campus. Never out of Ireland. Faces from the paths watched our every move. They would frown on too lively a conversation at this point. I decided not to question Gerard further.

Approaching the Cotter Tavern, the hearse slowed as the driver took a quick look at the large Guinness sign outside the door. A thirst coming up on him. A glance about caught all the other men licking their lips. Anticipating the free pint after the rites were done. Two stragglers ducked behind a van and shot through the pub door for a quick curer. Lourdes, they'd nicknamed the place. But some needed the remedy before the afflic-

---

tion. I could understand their disrespect. I was in need of a miracle myself.

Past Mount Saint Lawrence. I turned to Paddy. "Isn't the burial here?"

"I thought so too."

Kevin spoke up. "That place is filled. There's no more funerals to there since years ago. It's all shut up."

Over the moss-covered walls, the remembrances shut off except to diligent Sunday gardeners. Primroses and some delicate lilies requiring eternal attention. Through the gate the long avenues of monuments, mausoleums, stone angels, and marble headstones. Leading to the burial chapel that was only an empty shell, they said, because no Host had ever graced its tabernacle nor sanctuary light flickered, announcing the Holy Presence there. Just an empty vault where mourners used to pause for brief aspiration before rejoining the dampness outside the gates.

Up a short lane. Through a gate. A wide expanse of field stretching out before us with small black crosses numbered in neat white letters. A few fashionable headstones here and there.

A row of open graves. Laborers in fair isles and wellington boots turned down at the top. Looking sheepishly at the people. Roughhewn boards across the dark pit. The crowd taking up their positions.

A black limousine coasted to a stop ahead of all the carriages and small confusions. Priests poured out like drab insects. Brown, black; white frills. The main celebrant in stole and prayer book. Chanting as he came. The others muttering their responses. They really should not have been there at all. My father had been a bandsman, and bandsmen, like old soldiers, preferred the fife and drum and volley above the grave. But my mother had said that there would be nothing artificial. No embroidered uniforms and tinny old whistles. She said that in his last days he'd asked to have the priests there instead and not his diseased and spitting old companions. There was no changing her mind.

Again we gathered about into the tight circle of family with the successive waves of friends and blood relations spreading out in almost perfect symmetry. On the very outskirts, the rubbery diggers all forlorn. Waiting for the price of a pint. The priests at the center, circling the open wound of grave. Speaking of Israel and David and prophets and Most High.

The celebrant raised his right hand and made the sign of the cross. The coffin made a sudden heavy noise as it touched the earth below. My mother and sisters clutched one another. Paddy, Kevin, and I held them, our fingers tearing at their coats. The agony was high and I closed my eyes in an effort to shut out the pain. But it mounted and had its time with us. There was no avoiding the sound of the first shovels and the crack of the earth against the wood. We stood there suspended in an agony that only we knew and shared. Soon it was over. The priest in his *De Profundis* prayer sauntered off enmeshed in the ecstasy of his own voice. It was a relief.

With the sound gone, the women were easily persuaded toward the carriages and cars. We settled them securely among the unselfish neighbors. Maud said, before leaving, that there'd be sausages and rashers ready when we arrived home. Not to get too drunk. We weren't to make a show of ourselves. She wanted to take young Gerard with them, but I persisted. He would come with the men.

We walked back toward the grave. The laborers were already moving the boards to another location. They looked up as we approached. Two pounds apiece. The blessings of God on you, sir.

By the grave's head, young Gerard was lost in thought. As Paddy and I came toward him his lips trembled. But his whispers were not of the previous notes nor timbre. *Genial current of the soul. To meet the sun upon the upland lawn. Or draw his frailties from their dread abode.* Thomas Gray.

"Don't tell me the master taught you that, too?"

"Gray was the first poet we ever studied. I like the poem. I only say it on special occasions. It's not a good poem; it's much too loose. Grandpa Bon would want me to say it for him sometimes. But not always."

"Why not always?"

"Because sometimes it made him sad. Once he got very mad about it. He said that the poet really hated poor people and was laughing at them. Other times it would do nothing for him. I always waited for him to ask first, after he getting irritated that first time."

"I see. You like poetry very much?"

"No. Not especially. Only sometimes, too."

"This master, is he a Saint Joseph Brother?"

"No. He's married. He's not even Catholic. He's from England originally."

"English and Protestant?"

"Yes. And he's quite famous. He's been on the television once."

"Where did he graduate from? But I suppose you wouldn't know . . ."

"Yes, I do. He talks about it frequently. He even said that one of the Fellows of his college may come and talk to us on Auden. Some Jesuit priest from Campion Hall."

"Oxford?"

"Yes."

And I having him figured for a bogtrotter. Now I'd have to brush the dust off the secure texts and give your man another going over. The English intelligentsia. Sitting with their crossword puzzles and ploughman's sandwiches in pubs around noon. You'd sometimes have them pictured as testy clerks from Blackwell's or Woolworth's. Some of them dons, some tutors. But all intense as hell. Ivy on their walls, white flame within. No other life but learning.

"Jesus! You two will be here until doomsday talking about

them words. Haven't ye enough for one day? Let's get over there to the Cotter before they close for the afternoon." Paddy was impatient.

"We're all through," I said.

We were joined by Finn. "Where in the hell did you get off to?" I said.

"I was over at the auld fella's plot. 'Fair play to you,' said I to him. ' 'Tis the life you have.' It's only when the demons are dead that we can take the razz out of them. When they're alive you can't point a finger. Isn't that true?"

I supposed that it was at that. And we laughed at Finn's innocence all the way to the Cotter Tavern.

12

Thady

AS I HAD ANTICIPATED, the premises were crowded. Most of the company had come from our funeral and others. Some, though, were the pub's regular customers. Farmers. Several herders from the fairgrounds and their cronies. And there was that element that calls itself the literary class, of little education but much intrigue. I strayed my ears from our own talk of death to listen to some of the latter's words. One had broken prison in England and was on the lam. The speaker seemed more engrossed in his own rhetoric than in the plot of his yarn, so I quickly turned back to the chatter nearest me. Paddy was advising Kevin again with little result on Kevin's part. The last-minute admonitions. The leaving advising the left. I came to Kevin's aid. "I'll give him a good talking to before I leave," I said, winking to the boy behind Paddy's back. "I'll set a few things straight for him."

"He'll need that, Thady, if you'll do it. I don't have much time."

"When does your train leave?"

"Six. And it's three now."

"Today? I thought you had a few days to . . ."

"No. We're very busy this time of year. And when it's all said and done, it'll be the best in the long run. Getting back and away, I mean."

"I suppose you're right."

A short pause. Some empty glasses. Faces longingly and thirstily gazing our way. Paddy and I called two rounds. Words of appreciation everywhere. Even from alien mourners. But it was as it should have been. I had drunk at strangers' funerals before, often asking at the end of the night who it was we had buried.

"He had a masterful funeral," Paddy mused.

"Not unusual for a sandman, I'd guess," I said.

"Oh, more. This will be the talk of the parish and city for a long time," Finn cried.

Young Gerard interrupted. "Did you notice how all the lights turned green as we passed?" he said.

Paddy and Kevin looked at him partly in awe but moreso in confusion at being confronted by an absurdity surely attributable to the boy's age. Paddy was the first to answer. "They set them that way, lad," he said, and shifted to catch the bartender's attention again. Kevin's face betrayed only the new liveliness of the porter. A silly grin permanently fixed for all comments.

I looked at Gerard. He was disappointed at the reception of his words. I knew it. I could not have, at his age, made the same observation. I would have been more engrossed in the sentiment and wringing tear-cloth details. When does our age of reason come ambling in? I asked myself. In spurts and spasms. To Gerard, the funeral *did* count. It had stopped the mechanical world. Commanded it to halt. Whether through respect or edict. That was worth something. To freeze the solenoids of a busy city street. More than the drab knight of the cortege had ever managed to do in his life.

"That's the only time the lights will quit their antics," I said to Gerard.

"I know, Uncle Thady," he said. But his face fell a little. "It's sad, though, in a way. Isn't it? As if being dead was more important than waiting to cross the road."

I looked into this new face of all the formulations and compassions, and, for the slightest second, I felt envious of his position. If Maud ever knew his thoughts, she would flail his hide. And he might deserve it. Maybe it was that English master of his.

I called the bartender. "Give this man a shandy," I said.

"Jesus, Thady, Maud will have your life if she gets the whiff," Paddy cried.

"We'll hide him under our coats."

"We'll have to do more than that. Those fine words ye're talking won't lead Maud off the path."

Gerard sipped the shandy when it arrived. Then he fell into silence. He glanced from face to face as if absorbing the full nature of every one.

Paddy was saying, "What will you be doing after all this is over, Thaed? I mean, he left no will that we know of, God rest his soul, so you'll stand to come into a fair penny, being the eldest. And if there's a will that we don't know about, it'll all be the same anyway."

"I never gave that a thought."

"Well, it's something to consider. You might want to stay here."

"Surely you're not talking that kind of money? The sand was never so expensive a commodity."

110

"Not the sand. But when the Electric Supply Board paid off the fishermen and the sandmen, after damming the Shannon above Plassey, the Da got a fine nest egg. He never spent a penny of it. You knew him!"

"But how much could it be but a few hundred pounds?"

"Few hundred pounds, my arse! More like a few thousand!"

"Phew!"

"So you see, I'd be for sticking around. You're still an Irish citizen, right?"

"Yes."

"Well, why don't you take that fine education of yours and get on up there to the Brothers. They're always looking for teachers. Isn't that right, Ger?" He looked over at the boy.

"Yes, Uncle Paddy. And a lot aren't even Irish at all."

"That's right," Finn piped in. He had been conversing with a thin greasy man in the corner but was back now. "Christ, we'd have great times. We could really do the caper. Work all week. Off on the tear every night. Away every weekend. It'd be like old times."

Everybody laughed. Like a child's eyes, Finn's were afire, the idea presenting no hindrance, but a long progression of romances.

"Talk. Talk," I said. "Those Brothers wouldn't touch me in a month of Sundays. Old pagans are always liable to have relapses. I might catch fire in a class someday, and where would the fat be then? Right in the middle of the bloody fire. They'd find out about the marriage and the lot."

"But sure in the eyes of the Church you were never married. There'll be no record, since there was no marriage in the first place. By her laws, that is." I noticed how quickly he had added the little twist. No marriage. That stung. What it intimated created a sudden chill. Its suggestion of eternal isolation. Of old fires gone. I had loved Jenny as best I knew how, and though the years had left me marooned on the island of myself,

---

111

there were times such as this when the accidental remark made me wish for her. For a better past. For her arms about me, like long ago. Calling me her wild and lofty Irishman.

"No, Paddy. I could never hack it. My luck would be that they'd give me a religion class to teach. Then watch the bottom fall out of the po-pot."

"But Uncle Thady," Gerard said, "the masters never teach catechism or apologetics anymore. Only the Brothers are allowed to do that."

"There you are," Finn said.

"Well, there's really no way. I have a contract at home. I couldn't drop out on it."

"You could teach out the year back there, then come home. Or shit, just stay here. They're not going to be up in a huff if you say that your family needs you here. There's no end to the excuses you could come up with." Paddy was saying this, unaware of the contradictions inherent, if one was to take seriously his accusations spat out the night before. The dog never sees his own arse, as the Da used to say. But the idea did rather fascinate me, I had to admit. What if I did come back? I could manage on the money—they were making fifteen pounds a week when I left. Someone said about forty or fifty now. And accommodations? We could move out near my beloved Plassey. I would have a home at last. A place that was more than a room above an old woman's kitchen. How many times when the Nebraska mercury sank into its silver ball, and I sat shivering of flu or cold under the blankets, did I yearn for home? A home. Any home where warmth came in hot thick-creamed milk, flooded in pepper and butter, and the kind pinch of salt. I remembered crying once. Sat there with the tears streaming down. By myself. Not even the puttering about of old Gladys Kolowski downstairs. There would be solace here. I was almost certain of that. And what lay ahead in Nebraska? Nothing but more loneliness. And then one day the spasm or tumor that brought the death. Away in a cold unfriendly place, where no man knew my name. But . . . There was a lot to consider.

The prompting went on. I enjoyed a little this urging to stay. I told them that I would think about it. I should, at least, call the Brothers. No harm in an interview. A fellow could always try. All they could say was no. And there might be a cup of tea and a free scone thrown in.

The man of the house treated us to cold pig's head. I had not tasted "minister's face" in years, and the salt felt good on the portered saliva. Finn ate the tongue, gnawing the ox-red meat like a ravenous greyhound. Kevin liked the ear. Gerard and I cut into the yellow face meat. It was well seasoned and the aroma of smoke still hung on it.

After more Guinness we were obliged to relieve ourselves outside. The line was long, but the company of the men making their humorous comments to the one who happened to be on the stool made the wait pass. In. Out. Round about. And maybe back again if the job wasn't done properly the first time. A laughable circle of topcoats, arseholes, froth, and meat. And the passing of water.

There was more drink and even drinks beyond those drinks. Uncle Paddy would be late for his train, Gerard said, sipping now on a cordial. I concurred, looking at the clock and taking into account the rush to the house. And the good-byes —always an eternity in themselves. We decided to call a taxi, and when it arrived we piled into the small space, Gerard having to sit on my lap. The driver took the John Street route, avoiding the city rush at that particular time of the afternoon. We arrived at the house in minutes.

Maud and Sadie had packed Paddy's bags. They would kill us for not coming home, they said, to eat the rashers and eggs that lay dried on the hob. But soon all was forgotten in the flurry. Did he have his handkerchief? His beads? A drop of holy water? *Say hello and God bless to Gertie. And the children.* And

---

we were off, just Paddy and myself, Kevin having staggered to his bed.

We barely made it to the station on time, but the civil servant at the ticket counter, who happened to be a friend of Paddy's, rushed us through the terminal. The train began its slow tugging movements as soon as we lugged the suitcases aboard. Paddy filled up. "Well, Thaed, I suppose I won't see you again for a long time?"

"You'd never know. I've been thinking about the job here. There might be something to it."

"Why don't you think about it more. It'd be good for you."

"We'll see."

"Good-bye."

"Good speed."

"And to you, Thady, when you go. I'm sorry about last night. It was the death. I'm ashamed to . . ."

"No need for words. I understand. I needed it. I had it all coming. You should quit that interior decorating, though, and go in the ring."

We laughed the foolish senseless laughter of good-bye. In a matter of minutes we had clasped our hands together and rubbed faces. Then just as quickly Paddy was a speck of face on the serpent side of the departing carriages. "Only three carriages today," a porter remarked to another as I left the platform. "No one leaving anymore. There'll be no need for us after a bit." I decided to walk home. I thought of seeing Agnes, but I was too tired and the feeling was off me for the time being.

Once home, I was pampered and coaxed to eat sausages, rashers, and fried potatoes. I ate merely to please, but the fine hot tea was welcome. Neighbors and friends came and went. Outside the darkness fell. The fire was heaped high. Someone played, though at a very soft pitch, my father's John McCormack records on the old Victrola. Without introduction, the golden voice whispered out of the past. The lark in the clear air, swelling to ecstasy in its eucharist of song. Singing on this dark night with the bright birds of paradise.

I went to bed early and fell into a heavy sleep.

13

Thady

MY MOTHER was the first up the next morning. I awoke to find her by my bedside, holding a tray of food and poising the teapot to fill my cup. Having seen to my needs she sat down by the foot of my bed. We spoke about the wake. After I had gone to bed, she said, several neighbors dropped by and were disappointed at not seeing me. I'd have to see them all in turn. It wouldn't do to insult their feelings. Certain things had to be done. It was useless to argue. I agreed with her.

I looked at the clock on the mantel. It said ten. I had slept over twelve hours. Outside, the sun was well below the clouds. A good day. And I having to do so much. A telegram to Herb Jonassen. The call to the Brothers. The latter tensed me a little.

But hell, I thought, they could only say no. It was as simple as that. And Agnes. I wanted to see Agnes. Maybe have lunch or supper together. A little conversation. The more I thought of her the more I felt at ease inside. A nice warmth creeping through the cold. But I cautioned myself against the easy solace of a woman's affection. Still, there was no harm in a little joy, even if it was passing. My feet touched the floor. I was startled by its coldness. I should have brought my slippers, I thought.

On my way uptown I took the quays route. Waifs of children and mad sea gulls were everywhere. I joined with the youngsters in pelting the gulls with pebbles, but they were frightened of me and ran away to play elsewhere with their companions. What harm, I wanted to give them a few shillings for sweets, as visiting Americans had often done when I was a child.

My first port of call was the General Post Office on Lower Cecil Street. I passed small confectioners as they laid their wares across their counters. Bread vans scurried to and fro, one almost knocking me over. I tried to call to the driver, but he merely made an obscene sign with his arm and shouted for all to hear, "Fuck off, mister. Watch where you're going." I laughed it off to myself.

I thought that perhaps I should send Herb a night letter. It would be cheaper than the regular wire. But as I was about to go through the doors, I noticed a man scribbling at a writing desk. Why not!—an air letter. It would allow me to say so much more.

I found a desk and poised my pen. What to say to them? Herb Jonassen was a gentle and kind person. He genuinely cared for me. His wife, Sarah, too. I could not lie to them. There had been enough lies in the past. I began to write. I thanked them for their concern before my leaving. I gave the details of the funeral. I explained the matter of the inheritance and the possibility of a teaching position. But I would return to the college, I wrote, and finish the year. I was bright on the idea of their being able to visit me by Shannonside in the summers to come. I would write soon and give a definite date of my return.

Outside again, the sun blinded for a moment. I stood and looked toward the shadows. Suddenly I recognized a familiar face. But from where? I asked myself. I had it! He was the man who had discussed the tarnished lung at my father's funeral. I waved to him. He glanced in my direction. His face was vacant. He turned quickly, almost frightened, into a lane and was gone. I shrugged it off. He had recognized me but was too shy to confront me on his own and without a pint of Guinness before him. I laughed. I was a little put out but not enough to spoil the sunny day.

I walked briskly to the Dunmartin Hotel in Patrick Street. My first time as a guest in this quiet, rich place. One time, Finn and I pissed in their john, and right in the middle of the nervous ritual the bellhop captain discovered our rude presence and ejected our petrified frames into the street. Bellhops all smiles today. *Good-day, sir.* Courtesy on all sides. Irish crystal in showcases. Irish cabaret show advertised for Tuesday evenings. Irish baneens and linen paraded under the glass. Beleek china in delicate tableaus. Farmers and their shaggy wives sporting from the grill. I stepped into the conversation and soft tinkling sounds of the bar.

A few heads raised at my entry. Out of the fine smoke. Women in expensive tweeds. Men under moustaches. I made my way to the bar and straddled the stool nearest the lager cocks. The bartender all smiles. I considered a martini but chose a Guinness instead. *Guinness, sir?* I said yes, and he seemed surprised. The waitress went outside to fill the order. Faces all around me. A horsey female to the right. To my left, two gentlemen speaking rather authoritatively on some subject of importance. Not yet able to decipher their exact rapture. A few words. *Flat heads. No real skill. Highly industrialized areas.* Who or what on earth?

118

My drink arrived. The phone beside me tolled. A Mr. Nellington wanted. Some farmer across the room weaving through the chairs and low Formica tables. Eyes diverted. Attention captured. To be called in a bar could mean an emergency. The gentlemen to my left nodded. I smiled. We all gazed at the rough man picking up the telephone. *Hello. Oh, hello, Cyril. A terrible market altogether.* Relief spreading into the entire room. I felt a light touch on my shoulder.

"Excuse me. But are you British?" His face was puffed red. A man in his early fifties. Well dressed in Harris tweed.

"No. American."

"Splendid. Better yet. My friend Bertie and I are having a little discussion about darkies. I say that there's no room for them here in Ireland. He maintains that we cannot keep them out if we're to maintain face with the European community."

"Darkies?"

"Negroes and the like. Black men."

"Blacks."

"Yes. Yes."

His eyes blazed. Turning his large jowls to the other, quieter and younger, man. "What did I tell you. These Americans have had their fill of the lot. Lazy bunch. Never a full day's work in any of them."

"Yet one cannot forget, of course," I said, "the bales of cotton which produce the clothes nearest to our skin and also the sexual superiority of these people. Those lingering reminders make all the difference."

I saw the red one squirm in his clothes. My syntax was jumbled but the key words had done the trick. The quiet man smiled. He knew my game. "The gentleman's right, you know, Cecil," he said. "These people are essential to . . ."

"Essential be damned! I've seen the darkies in India. Couldn't make a pot of tea to satisfaction. Foreigners, all of them!"

His eyes darted nervously. Perhaps there would be a real

emergency soon. I rose from my stool. The clock said three. It was time to put in my call to the Brothers. Walking toward the door, I caught the reflection of Cecil in the mirror. He was puffed up like a turkey cock. I laughed, but I felt sad. Somehow, my success with him had been blighted. I was playing foolish and pointless games.

The lobby was crowded. I found a bellhop and asked to be directed to the telephones. He said downstairs. I pushed through the arms and shoulders and reluctant buttocks. On the stairs I noticed that the carpet was worn right through to its padding in places. I was disappointed. The Dunmartin Hotel had always been the most prominent and revered fixture in our town. Almost instinctively, I closed my eyes for a brief moment.

The telephone kiosks were situated to the left of the lower stairs. The hotel operator requested the desired number and pointed to an open booth. I waited. Her face showed no emotion or indication of response. Sitting there I imagined the telephone ringing in the shadows of the headmaster's office. The sound circling the room. The hand reaching slowly for the instrument.

The operator was beckoning. I lifted the receiver and said good afternoon. A deep country voice at the other end asked my business. It was a Brother Cleary, the headmaster. I felt for a moment that I was again in my old corduroys, sitting in the parlor, waiting for my schoolboy punishment. But I reminded myself of my equal stand now. Still, I was afraid. I opened the conversation awkwardly by stating that I was a past pupil of his school. His attitude changed. He wanted to know the years I had attended. The men on the hurling teams? Had we ever won the Munster College final when I was there? Was Mick Ginty playing then? Who was the headmaster in my time? And so it went, all my past unfolding.

I was caravanned back over the years by his voice. I tried to remain aloof but found myself, instead, blurting out the old memories of battle cries, masters, games, and retreats. We must have a longer chat, he said. Could I come for tea? he asked. I said Friday. Before he could arrange the time, I said that I should mention that I was after a teaching position at my old school. He was suddenly silent. But his voice came across the line after the pause. It was enthusiastic. Why certainly, Thady, he said. We can see what we have next year. You'd be no small asset to our staff. What with all those degrees and experiences. I'll talk to the Brother Superior and put in a good word for you. Three o'clock then it is. Good. I was astounded. I thanked him, but my words were jumbled. He laughed at my excitement.

Outside, the sun was falling easily along the lanes and alleys, making its ever-rising tide of shadows on the walls and sills. I was happy as I stood on the threshold of the hotel. I looked about for a familiar face. A pint with all the usual conversation would be the ticket. But there was no one on the street who knew me. I decided to head for Maud's home. Gerard would surely be back from school. I would take him to Kelly's and wait there for Agnes to finish work. I went back into the hotel and had the bellhop call for a taxi.

14

Thady

THE NEIGHBORS around Bishop Street had not lost their curiosity. They looked up from their sweeping and child chastising as the taxi drew to the curb. But having recognized me and placed my face within the tapestry of ordinariness, they went back to their duties.

I knocked on the door. Maud opened it in a matter of moments. Then suddenly she became anxious for the state of her house. I shouldn't have dropped in without letting her know, she said. And she not having a drop in the house to offer me. She was really upset. "Jesus, Maud," I said. "I'm your brother, not a visiting cardinal. And the way it looks from today, I may become a permanent fixture around the place."

"How's that?" she cried.

"Well, I had a little chat with the headmaster at Saint Joseph's. He thinks that I may be his man to teach English next year. I have an appointment with him on Friday. He invited me to tea. How's them apples?"

"Oh, Thaed, that's wonderful. And after all them years away. And all the sadness. That'd be great for Mama to have you home. And for us all." She was excited. She came across the floor and kissed me.

"Wait now. It's not final yet, you understand."

"It will be. It will be."

"I might even have Ger in my class."

"Oh."

We sat close in against the table and watched silently, for awhile, the children playing in Old Tannery Place. At length, noticing the quietness of the house about us, I asked where her children were. She said that her husband's people had come into town for the day and were treating the children to the carnival rides in Jack Naughton's field.

"Gerard, too?" I asked, thinking him a little too sophisticated for such enjoyments.

"No, no," she said. "He was up at the crack of dawn today. The school had a football game in Charlesville. Munster College's Cup or something. He won't be back until late tonight. And what harm, he didn't have a thing to eat before he went out the door. Oh, the youngsters these days, Thady!"

"He's a very smart boy. Do you know that?"

"Do I know it? Amn't I scourged from books and engines and God-knows-what-else lying around the place? You should see his room!"

"I'd like to, really."

"Wait'll after tea, I'll take you up."

"You should be proud of him, from all I hear."

"Thady, we always feel proud. It's *grateful* I am."

"Grateful?"

"For his health. Sure, he nearly died when he was a little child. Jimmy and I were certain that we'd lost him. But he's as healthy as a workhorse now."

After tea Maud led me up the banistered stairway to Gerard's room. His door was unlocked. This surprised me, as I expected secrecy in one so sensitive. The room was bright. As for furniture, it contained merely a bed, a chair, and a small bureau-type desk. Several shelves were arranged along the walls. These were neatly stacked with books. I read some of the titles. A collection of poems by Kinsella. A criticism of Auden's work. Paperback plays from various periods. A minuscule sampling of Byron. And at least a hundred airplane magazines!

"What does he do with the airplane literature?" I asked.

"He builds models from them and flies them out by Park, somewhere."

I remembered that only the rich enjoyed such indulgences when we were children. And here in Gerard's room all the old envies were paid for. What would he go out into the world despising? What on earth were richer children flying these days? Certainly not full-scale models! Still, there had to be a scaling, didn't there? A different kind of scaling. Or was it that only dire deprivation brought about that artificial charting within?

The little room seemed complete. We left it and went down into the kitchen. The warm hearth was inviting as I looked into the darkness beyond the windows.

"Why don't you stay awhile, Thady," Maud said. "I'll make some more tea, and we can sit down there by the fire and talk about old times."

I thought about her loneliness and how trying it must be to have one's husband work so far away. Her eyes were big for attention above her belly filled with child. It would be too convenient to wallow in the past. To stay and talk. And I had to admit to myself, in all honesty, that I was eager to leave. Restless and awkward in my own sister's company. But it was the truth. "Well, Maud," I said, "I should be getting home. We must leave some of those memories for all the winter nights ahead."

"I suppose you're right," she replied. She kissed me again on the cheek and went after my coat. We promised to have tea like this again before the week was out. But I was to tell her in advance, she said, so that she could get something special in the house.

I pulled my coat about me as I stepped into the light rain that was coming up from the river. Perhaps if I could find a telephone. But then I would be obliged to go back inside and wait for the cab. A pub. That would be ideal. I walked briskly in the direction of Deegan's. I looked forward to a drink, too. And there was Agnes. I had to find her and explain my failure to show up the night before.

Deegan's was practically empty. A few dockers drinking at the end of the bar began whispering as I entered. Perhaps they recognized me. But I couldn't be sure. As soon as I took a stool, the proprietor approached me. His head popped out from under the counter like a ferret exploring the sky. "Good afternoon, Mr. Quinlan," he said. "I've been meaning to get ahold of you in the matter of the other night. You see, there was a share of glasses and sundry items broken. Mind you, it's not that I begrudge young fellas their wildness, but I must insist . . ."

"How much did it come to?"

"Well, I wasn't quite . . ."

I took my wallet from my pocket. I had ten large blue notes tucked under the leather flap. I looked into my accuser's greedy eyes. He would surely overcharge, so I decided to beat him to it. I placed five bills on the counter. "Will this cover it?" I said. "Or will you want to give me change?"

His hand shot out and grabbed the bills. "Just fine," he cried. "Just fine, Mr. Quinlan. You even have a free drink coming."

His gift of whiskey and ale was welcome. As he hoisted the dripping glasses onto the counter, I asked where Agnes might be. He said that it was her evening off. "She's at home on a night like this, surely," he said.

I nursed my drink, watching the dangerous eyes of the black-faced men at the end of the counter. They were silent under my stare. I felt their hostility and wondered if one might come down the bar and begin again the violence of two nights ago. The owner standing me a drink had not helped matters. Their lives rotated between dark points of raucous laughter and sterilizing pain. Dangerous places with no high hand of reason in between. But they remained seated, merely looking into my face. I drained my glass and asked the proprietor to call a taxi.

Within minutes the hooter sounded. I walked through the barrels and sawdust. The taxi hooted again.

I instructed the hackney to drive by Sheep Street. He was annoyed but complied. Agnes's windows were black. Even the scullery light in the back was out. I could not guess where she was. At the chapel? Bingo? Her family's house? I turned to the driver and said, "Higher Brazil Street, please."

On Mary Street the rain washed itself along the shiny crystal pavement. A few old people ambled through the squalls of rising rain to reach their milk shops or pubs. A solitary child watched the lights of our car from a lighted window. I waved, but his curtains fell and he retreated into the yellow-ochred warmth of his home. Watching the rain, I thought. A delightful diversion.

My mother and Sadie were at the door to greet me. For an instant I half expected to see my father's face appear, too, in the light behind. Once inside, my mother reached and took my coat. What a dreadful night, she said. And after such a lovely morning. Yes, Sadie said. There are ships delayed and some small boats came loose from their moorings down at the docks. A most awful night, God bless us and save us!

Within minutes I was out of my damp clothes and sitting

by the fire in my robe. Outside in the kitchen, Sadie was cooking a beefsteak and onions. I sat back and let the dancing heat scorch my face.

Suddenly, my mother called from the bedroom, where she was heating the sheets with an iron. "Did you get the letters?" she cried.

"What letters?" I said.

"Some letters came for you today. They're on the mantel. I'll be right out."

"That's okay. I'll find them."

I stood and scanned the mantel. There they were by the smiling china dogs. Two letters. Both from Herb Jonassen. Mailed the day of my departure. Once torn open, the envelopes revealed two additional letters. One, a note from a girl I had met at Oxford and who was now living with a friend in New York. She would try to see me in the summer on her way to New Mexico. The other displayed all-too-familiar handwriting. The contents would be no surprise to me. More pleas. More admonitions. I was not disappointed. I held the sheet to catch the fire's light.

Dear Thady,

I am writing again concerning someone who is very dear to both of us— Bernie. He will be five years old in a few weeks, and over the greater part of those years he has come to consider Johnny his father. Soon he will be asking why his last name is Quinlan and ours is Soderfield. Johnny loves Bernie and wants to adopt him. I would like to see that, as they both have a real affection for one another. We have no children of our own, as you know.

My life is different now, Thady, from what it was when we were together. My husband has none of your fire. I sometimes miss what it was that kept you going, kept you trying to make the final impression on someone somewhere who was a stranger to me. I even have to admit that I enjoyed the perverse role you imposed on me

---

127

—that of first being the end of your hopes and then almost immediately becoming the means toward other further goals. I was wrong, though, about you. I was not, as I used to say, the one who made your success possible for you. Someone else would eventually have fallen for your special brand of charm; or, becoming more confident in your new surroundings, you would have shed your uneasiness and created your own world. You were and are of Ireland, Thady. Your sickness was born there somewhere, and had you stayed, it would have come to light and been accepted as the norm by those other men and women about you. But now it is tied to a thousand other strains, and God alone knows what it will turn you into before it's done, unless you break the shell and escape. Please begin by giving me our child to raise as a healthy human being who will thrive on love and not complexity and torment.

Think it over, Thady. Let's set someone else's life right— even if we made a total wreck of our own.

Best wishes,
Jenny

The gall. The utter gall of her. To ask that I relinquish my son to an inferior blob of flesh. *My* sperm. *My* blood. *My* son. But he was linked to me by more than that. All the past. All gone before. Everything to come. Tied to him in an inexorable silver call of race and mosaic of memory. To cut him off would be to make him a floating ship of no origin. To make him the heir of a cardboard and inane world. A man is nothing without his past, my father used to say. For Bernie to be raised in such a manner and not know this land, this terrible, sweet, fecund Ireland, was intolerable to me. I threw the letters on the table.

My mother, coming into the kitchen, said, "What's all the fuss, Thady, love?"

"Oh, nothing. Just that bloody wife of mine again."

"What does she want now?"

"Go ahead and read the letter." I picked up the envelope and handed it to her.

Her eyes searched for the beginning, and with each jerk of her face she seemed to swell and fester. The cheek, she said under her breath several times. When she had finished, her face seemed drained of blood, and again, as at my father's funeral, I saw the fishlike texture of her skin. She was, for an instant, frightening in her fit of anger. Suddenly her compassion came swarming as she held my head in her arms. "This would never happen, I can assure you, Thaed, love, if she were here. She'd be in the county jail for all she's done. The little bitch, to be scalding you like this! The very cheek of her trying to break what Almighty God destined to remain together."

She wiped her hands on her bib. "If only you could get the child here. Bring him over for a holiday and never let him back. Do you think for one minute that the Irish Catholic government would let a child go back to a mother that is a pagan hussy?"

With that she was gone. I thought on her words. Bernie was still part of me no matter where he was kept. It all required more thought. I sat back in the chair. I watched the lights on the ceiling and listened to the sounds of the river. They were no longer robust, but the mere chirping noises of rats and otters. There was peace when night fell like this. Locked inside out of the rain. With the eternity of silence. So far from Nebraska's joined phases of sleep and anxiety.

I awoke frequently during that night. My thoughts were of the boy and his mother's words. And of my own feelings and of my mother's words.

15

Thady

SMALL PATCHES OF FOG obscured the bright sun on Wednesday morning as I caught the Ballinacurra bus to Punch's Cross. I had decided that the small luxury of a rented car would not be an extravagance. I was tired of hackney cars. Renting would give me the freedom to come and go as I pleased. I would be able to see the countryside, too. My first stop, of course, would be Plassey. Sitting in the cozy double-decker bus, the conductor up front counting his change, the driver roaring then slowing the engine, I felt excited.

At the Cross I was amazed to see the changes in this part of the city. Very little had differed within the old walls. But here was change. New housing schemes were running south, then west, then north. The roads were aflurry with farmers and businessmen making their impatient ways into the city. At the garage section of O'Brien's Rental, five cars and a small bus were waiting to be gassed.

At the main office I was introduced to a Mr. Seoirse O'Brien, the manager's son. He asked the usual questions and then looked into my face.

"Were you ever at Saint Joseph's?" he said.

"Yes. About ten years ago."

"I knew I recognized the name. It's a small world. I was a year behind you. I remember your poems in the paper."

"A small world is right."

The recognition made all the difference. I was given a lower seasonal rate than was in effect at the time. When he came to the car classification, he gave me a model from his top group and charged me for the lowest category. I couldn't thank him enough. Old schoolboys must stick together, he said, and politely excused himself into the glass of his office. He waved as I drove out of the lot and into the stream of traffic.

I was uneasy at first driving on the left side of the road. At the Crescent a man ran right in front of me, and I almost hit the railings below the Daniel O'Connell Monument. But by Shannon Street I was in better form. And at the Dunmartin I was confident enough to look across and catch a glimpse of the tall elegant girls entering the hotel for their morning coffees.

Athlunkard Street was almost deserted. I pulled into the space outside Deegan's and, having locked the car, made my way inside. At first the darkness blinded me. I looked around. There was nobody in the bar, it seemed, but noise was coming from somewhere behind the counter. I stepped silently to one of the stools and leaned over. I could see a girl's back as she scrubbed the wooden floor beneath her. Was it Agnes? I couldn't be sure. It could be the owner's wife. I took the chance. Reaching for a rumpled newspaper that lay across one of the stools, I rolled it into a baton. I leaned across the counter and swacked hard. There was a scream. I waited nervously. The hair. The face. It was Agnes.

"Thady Quinlan! I'll murder you! You gave me the fright of my life!" Then her face burst into laughter.

"You must be eternally vigilant."

"At eleven o'clock in the morning?"

She wiped her hands on a white towel and poured me a large Paddy. Her eyes were sparkling and delighted. "So tell me," she said, "where have you been? Off with all those swanky blondes uptown? I thought I'd never see sign nor light of you again. And you so eager the other night." She pursed her lips.

"I'm sorry about that. I wasn't in my right mind."

"I'm just teasing you, Thady. I'm a grown woman. I understand. I would have loved to have had you in, but the old biddies around my place have mouths as big as Christmas."

"I came by last night to see you."

"Here?"

"Yes. And the house, too. All was in darkness there."

"Oh, my God! What harm, I spent the whole night watching a stupid picture at the Rialto."

"Damn. I'm never going to get to take you out unless I kidnap you."

"Well, fine sir, I'm off today and open for suggestions. We could go for a walk."

"How about a drive?"

"You have a car?"

"Just got it. How about Plassey?"

"That'd be just great, Thady. I won't be out of here until nearly twelve, and by the time I make us a few sandwiches and clean up, it'll be nearly one o'clock. Would that be all right?"

"Fine."

"Are you sure?"

"Certainly."

We talked and laughed for nearly another forty minutes. I told her of my appointment with the headmaster at Saint

Joseph's. She was elated. There would be grand times ahead, she said. Had I told Finn yet? She would tell him the first thing. Finally she cried, "Thady Quinlan, I'm going to have to run you out of here. I'll never be ready if you keep me company like this. Lovely company, mind you, but the work will never get done."

"I'll leave. I can take a hint."

She opened the door for me, and, as I turned to go, she squeezed my side. "One o'clock. You're sure?"

"I'm sure."

I started the car and drove down the mall. It had been a long time since I remembered being so lighthearted. I decided to drive through the town and while away the remaining time. I should get to know it all again—the lanes, the corners, the old walls. Especially if I was going to make it my permanent home in the fall.

16

Thady

THE ONE O'CLOCK HORN was blowing as I pulled into the Abbey common and eased the car through a gang of brawling boys, only to be immediately confronted by a herd of sheep and cows scattering in every direction under the ineffectual tutelage of a wild drover. He waved to me as I passed and made a motion of desperation. I smiled. He probably knew my family.

Agnes's door was ajar. I parked the car close against the wall and unlocked the trunk. When she came to the door she was all smiles and pride. She wore a bright yellow dress sashed by a band of black ribbon. Her dark eyes seemed to dance like darting shadows. I helped her with the picnic basket, placing it close against the soft blankets she had first handed me. They would act as a buffer and prevent any breaking of the precious jars and bottles. All was set. Everything in its place. Not an irregular strand in the whole caravan.

We decided to take the Annacotty road to Plassey. It was completely asphalted and would eliminate any scratching of the car or walking through the fields and swamps surrounding the road's end of the other route. Of course, in the other direction there was always the delicious reward for the trouble, as one staggered, torn and hot, into Jack Noonan's pub, there to sit under the cool trees and sip shandies, brought foaming by Jack to your table. This could wait, though. Perhaps another day. Sunday or Monday of next week. Plassey, like a magic crystal, brought to itself a new image by reason of every route taken to its core of sand islands and ruined castles. The paths along the canal banks wound their ways through reeds and tall grass and gave the notion of a perilous journey through devouring undergrowth to that place of light and placidity. The Corbally road tunneled under the trees of Blackwater, deep into the blackthorn core of darkness and fright, only to bound in whorls of windfall brightness onto the even altar fields below Castle Bridge. Our way by Annacotty was not without its romance either. The road turned beyond the small village into lanes of thick briar and furze bushes. At a sharp corner in the boreen, the hedgerow separated to reveal a tiny stretch of scoured field where bicycles could be parked or cars set under the heavy chestnut foliage, safe from the sun. We had often taken that road as children and walked in terror past Mount Shannon House, scarred and blackened by the fires of the Troubles, long before our times. But all that was long ago. Perhaps Plassey and the roads to it had changed. I would see very soon.

As we turned beyond Groody River, I looked across at Agnes, who had been until then basking in the warm sunshine, half-asleep, her face smiling contentedly.

"Sun too hot?" I said.

She looked into my face. "No," she said. "It's just lovely.

135

Thank you." Her hand touched mine, and she snuggled into the seat.

"What do you remember of Plassey?" I said.

"Oh, that it was always beautiful, free, and without a shred of responsibility to it."

"But particularly, I mean."

"Well, as children we'd go there of a Sunday morning. The whole family would bring some little thing to eat. Brawn or ham or sausage. My mother, God rest her, would spread a big white cloth across the grass. Oh, my God, how we'd eat! I think that we had stomachs without end."

"When did you stop going up there?"

"When I started work. There was never any time. And then my father, before he passed away, took a dislike to Plassey."

"What do you mean?"

"He said that it was the graveyard of the Shannon. That was when the fishermen and sandcotters sold their rights to the river and the government took the water for the Shannon Scheme Dam at Ardnacrusha. It left the river at Plassey as only a channel gulley. I'm sorry, Thady. I didn't mean to criticize your father, God rest him."

"That's all right. I know they sold out. It will be interesting to see the water now. When I knew it, it was swollen and distended like a great woman in labor."

"What did ye do up there? Picnic?"

"Not always. You see, my father and brother worked the river east as far as Sandy. I never went along. My job was to stay near the jetty in the town and wait for them at a certain time of the evening. Then I'd made the deliveries of sand all over Limerick."

"You didn't go to Plassey too much, then?"

"Yes. But not by sandcot. My mother was dead set against that."

"How, then?"

136

"Bicycle. I was a member of the rowing club. We practiced around six and my father and brother didn't arrive back until near eight o'clock. So I had the whole morning and afternoon off, in the summer, to explore and galavant. I spent almost every day in the woods across from Sandy."

"All by yourself?" Her lips were moist. She was joking.

"There were *some* girls. One called Ann. There was another—Deirdre something."

"Deirdre O'Brien and Ann Burke. I know them well."

"Are they still around?"

"They're around all right, but they wouldn't give one the time of day. All airs and graces. They married well. It must have gone to their heads."

"Have they forgotten where they came from?"

"You're right, Thady. But sure they have nothing else but their snobbishness. No more of the old friends left to them."

"I'd like to walk in on them someday."

"You would, and they'd probably wrawk you into bed with them. And I'd kill them both!" She laughed, and her white teeth made her hair so much darker. I leaned across and kissed her cheek. She was not angry. "Thady Quinlan," she said. "If you don't look out, we'll all be killed."

We were past Annacotty now. Agnes began to sing softly. Hers was an old voice, not in age, but in tenderness. I listened to the lilt of it as we bumped over the ruts and holes of the disjointed road and out under the heavy trees and spots of fleeting sunlight.

The opening to the boreen seemed no different than before, except that a small gate had been strung across its mouth. But it was a latch affair and had no lock. The spring rains had left the road in a soft bog of green and black mud. I drove fast at first, hoping to be out of the swamp as soon as possible, but several lurches of the car convinced me that my impatience, if I wasn't careful, could become expensive. Softened by my sudden failure to control, I set the stick in high gear and we ambled awkwardly but safely through the mud. Soon we were onto dry tar, leaving the tracks of our experience behind us. I doubted if I would ever be able to clean the car. It would take a professional to free the thick mud and caked slime.

I parked in the same area where I had so often in the past ditched my rusty bicycle. The smoothness of the ground seemed different, worn down to the fine hardened clay. Through the trees the turrets and gables of Mount Shannon House were outlined against the bright cumulus. I felt a slight shudder run through me. Was it the old fear from childhood or the memory of the many legends spun about this place? We had often skirted hedges in one jump, when someone swore to seeing dark figures fleet through the courts or peer from the upper windows of the house, gazing eternally at the stables where it was said that the children and horses burned, their flesh, or what remained of it, becoming one in the terrible heat. Wild improbable stories. I looked askance at the ivy and long shadows before climbing the stile. Agnes was silent.

"Is anything the matter?" I asked.

"No," she said. "It's just that place. It gives me the creeps."

"I don't think that I've quite forgotten it myself."

"The shameful things that happened there. My God, the cruelty of even our own."

"It was ours before the English came though, Agnes. You must remember that."

"Ours or not, no one has the right to hurt another person. Do they?"

"I suppose not." I did not completely agree, but the probing of possibilities could only taint our day.

As I spoke I heard voices from the direction of the house. They were soon identifiable. Several boys were balancing themselves on the eastern parapets while their friends shouted encouragement from the ground.

Once past the mansion, we made our way through the first

woods, finding the paths clearly marked and worn. Small bridges had been built across the various streams. There were new cabins here and there, but not enough to change the fine austerity of the thick green places. In one section the branches of chestnut had been broken, though ever so carefully, so that the splintering light could fall on the rise of a small hillock clearing. We stood in the warmth. Down below lay the second woods. Agnes wanted to picnic there, but I was anxious to go deeper. It wasn't far to the real Plassey. There was no need to cheat ourselves of the best.

The second woods were untouched except for a small pump-house. But that had always been there. We had often thrown stones against it and listened to the echoes drift across the river. Soon the grass and undergrowth became thickly interwoven. I noticed threads pulled on my sweater. Agnes wiped her face several times. Perhaps we should have stayed in the sunny patch, I thought. But I kept on. The reward would be worth all the pain.

As I had anticipated, the density was only temporary. We were approaching the light again in a matter of minutes. I could hear the sounds of the main river. The rush of water over stones and against the leafy islands. We were in a dark trench for several seconds, then up a thorny rise and into the brightness.

Instantly we were in that world stolen away by the necessity of separation but always bright and glistening in the mind's eye. It was as though the years, despite the constant reviewing of each detail, had dulled and numbed the vision ever so slightly. And now the trees, the rushes, the falls, and the white sand burst into my consciousness, brighter than they had ever been before, each thing in itself a vital part of that mosaic clutched by me in the throng of all the dissuasions. There was no other place like this.

Agnes stood as I dropped the basket in excitement and ran to the water's edge. In seconds my shoes were off, and I was wading and swirling about like a child. I splashed water on

Agnes, and she screamed that she was going to get me. White sand suddenly rained down everywhere. I was covered in fine powder. She threw some more. I moved against the heavy mass of freezing water. My feet finally touched the firm ground underneath. And we were off through the fields like tinkers, shouting wild threats at one another in the clear air. My bare feet. Her long golden legs under the sun.

After several unsuccessful chases, I declared a peace, and Agnes passed me a lantern reed as a token of the pact. She then dragged me by the hand back to a small clearing below the bank where stones were piled. "Now, Thady Quinlan," she said. "Let's hope that you're more successful at lighting the fire than catching me."

"I could have caught you. I was being kind."

"I'm sure."

I looked across at her. She was truly beautiful. She was part of this place. Part of the green and blue and white.

I searched about for wood that might have dried out or had been sheltered from the heavy spring rains. It was hard to find. I gathered twig after twig, realizing that they would burn in one glorious flash of flame, but have little sustaining power. I needed heavy reliable bark or a log of dead wood to keep the fire burning for at least an hour or so. But everywhere the fragments were soaked and rotting. I decided to at least bring back my collection of thorny twigs.

To my surprise, when I returned Agnes had a blazing fire going. I dropped the twigs in a disorderly pile.

"That's a fine how-do-you-do," I said. "I'm out there searching my heart out, and you're here warming yourself by a bonfire."

"Serves you right for chasing me. You're being punished."

"Where on earth did you get the wood?"

"I used some splinters and sticks that I brought along. I also found a damp log to keep in the heat."

"Agnes the scoutmaster."

"Don't stand there gaping. Help keep the fire going. Dreaming about hot tea won't *make* hot tea."

"Yes, sir!" I leaned down and kissed her. She touched my face with her hands.

At the water's edge I rinsed the kettle. I could see clearly the small movements of the green moss beneath the surface. Occasionally, a flash of silver would reveal hordes of minnows moving in one body, the shadows frightening them into flight. There were eel fry, too, squirming under the rocks. Farther out, when the light was right, I saw perch basking in the sun, their eyes sterile and fixed. I tried to wade out into the deep water, but the cold stopped me. The sun had not succeeded in lifting the chill. I was obliged to turn back. As I reached the shore, I noticed a small boat anchored nearby. I lay flat in its bow and paddled slowly into the deep water. I rinsed the teapot several times before returning to the shore.

Agnes had the fire in a fine glow. She nestled the teapot between two narrow rocks. "We'll have the tea in no time," she said.

"If I had a rod, we'd have fish, too. The river is swarming with them."

"They're just coarse fish."

"I'd eat anything."

"The river is too swollen with them. I don't know. It isn't natural. It's different below the city. The tide makes them move or something. I really don't know what it is. I'd just be afraid of them here. I don't really know why."

"Oh, women!"

"Go ahead and tease. See if I care if you're poisoned or not."

The cold water of the river would take some time to boil, I decided, so I placed a blanket against the bank and stretched out on it. The sun was warm on my face. All around, the air hummed with birds and the sounds of small life. Agnes was

141

busy unwrapping the packages. I closed my eyes and in seconds must have drifted off to sleep.

I awoke to the sound of voices in the distance. Agnes was beside me. She, too, had been dozing, it seemed. We looked toward the woods. Though we were hidden from view, we could still catch glimpses of the approaching crowd.

"Who is it?" I said.

"Just a group of children on a hike," she said. "They're the only ones who come here anymore."

"Will they see us, do you think?"

"They might. But sure, it's no harm. They'll mind their own business."

Agnes turned out to be right. In a surge of excitement they carried their voices over the iron bridge and into the deep grass and trees. We watched them disappear, first a bright jumper, then a gay hat, then no sign at all of them. Like elves they had come and gone, whisking away their gay streamers into the nothingness.

For a few moments we lay under the blankets. I could feel the closeness of Agnes's body. Her eyes were closed and she seemed to be musing on some memory or thought and keeping it intact, safe from spoil. She moved under the blankets. Her firm breasts against my chest.

"You smell so nice, Thady," she said.

"Just cologne. One needs a lot of it in Nebraska."

"Is it really that bad, or are you making it up for me?"

"Worse."

"I wish that you didn't have to go back so soon."

"I'll be back."

"Are you sure?"

"Why? I'll have no trouble. The Brother was more sure than not on the phone."

"Still and all, I have a feeling that something will come up and I'll not see you again."

"What pessimism! Jesus! I'll swear before a high magistrate that I'll be back by September. Will that convince you?"

She seemed startled by the sudden jolt of my voice. Perhaps I had sounded more vehement than I intended. I had only been joking, taking her fear and expanding it into an absurdity. "I didn't mean to frighten you," I said. "I was only joking."

She smiled. I put my hand under the fold of the blanket. The flesh of her back was warm. I stroked it gently. She moaned slightly and lifted her face to my mouth. I looked along the banks. They were deserted. The children were fields away by now. A solitary swan drifted across the river and disappeared into the rushes at the other side. There was no fear. I kissed her neck and moved my lips along her shoulders. Suddenly, she pulled away. "Can't you kiss my face, Thady?" she said.

"What the . . ."

"Kissing me like that makes me helpless. I don't want to be like an animal. I want to be kissed and be able to kiss back, and then let the rest of me follow or wait or do whatever it does after my eyes and lips have decided. Don't Americans kiss on the face anymore?"

"Why do you say that?"

"One time at a ceilidhe, I was caught under the mistletoe with an American soldier, and right there on the floor he started to run his lips all over my neck and shoulders."

"That's not unusual. He probably just acted as if he were at home."

"You mean that just there and then, without responsibility or even knowing someone, to actually try and excite that person?"

I looked at her for awhile. I had met girls before whose delicate innocence and adamant refusals lasted only until the second date, and who then, having estimated your permanency, yielded like field cattle in heat. But Agnes was making no such demands. It was all absurd. She was simply asking to be kissed on the mouth!

"If you don't want to. I mean if it offends . . ."

"I didn't say that at all, Thady. Now you're hurt."

"No. In your way it may be wrong, but I have different ideas," I said, unable to halt the creeping disgust. "I have given up all that rot about dirty filthy little sins that smell in the eyes of God. Jesus! How many times I heard that rigmarole."

"Nobody said anything about dirty, Thady. You're twisting words. I just asked to be looked at as a girl and kissed as one, not plied like an old piano that anyone can play a drill on."

"And I was plying you?"

"Weren't you?"

"I was doing what any natural living thing would do."

" 'Thing'?"

"Goddamn it, Agnes! You're caught up in the whole old lie. Everything is a sin. This is a sin. That is a sin. God knows what the hell else is a sin."

"And now nothing is a sin?"

"That's right. I do as I please. I answer to nobody. I am high, low, between—all at my own whim. Given the opportunity, I would have made love to you, because you are attractive. Because you, more than anybody I've met in a long time, appeal to me. I can't be more straightforward than that."

"Well, to me, Thady, there are sins. And the sins are not in the things themselves, but in the duty of one person to another. You can't go about taking this and throwing the other away. Call it what you want, natural or whatever you like. Sin is that without a shred of responsibility, you take your pleasure, and not as much as a 'how are you?' for anyone."

"There's no use talking. The whole thing's wrecked anyway. It all boils down to the old and the new. The owl and the nightingale."

"What?"

"Nothing."

"Thady, if it didn't go deeper than what you're saying, everybody would be like spindrift. We'd all be very fine under the sun, like now, or in the dark corners of little lounges. But where would we be in the mornings? Or after waking up in the night, our hair all out like a witch's? Sure, God, nobody would love us or care about us if things were all so casual as you say. We'd despise one another at the sight of the first bad habit."

Her voice broke and she began to sob. I felt foolish sitting there, my face red with anger. I pressed her against me. She was chilled, and her skin felt rough to the touch. I moved my hand under her breast. She tightened for a moment, then put her arms about my neck, moving the arch of her body into mine. I loosened the straps of her dress. Underneath, her flesh was white like that of the schoolgirls of long ago. She offered no resistance, but clung to me in a desperation that frightened me at first, but soon gave way to a gentleness I had long forgotten existed. I kissed her on the lips, knowing that in her there was no selfishness, no pain, and no demands. The feeling was strange but calm to me.

Afterward I lay back against the bank. The wind had died and the water reflected the trees again in clear outline. It was safe to be under the rough blanket.

I heard their voices before seeing the gay smiling heads pop and bubble out of the woods. Their laughter grew in increasing spirals of delight until they were directly above us, but almost as suddenly died as they sang their silly-nilly songs and marched off in disarray to their mothers in the city. Agnes kissed me. They had seen us this time, I was sure, but had chosen to leave us to ourselves.

The teapot began to boil. Agnes stirred. "I'll make you some hot tea to take away the chill."

"I'm warm," I said.

"Maybe too warm," she teased.

When the tea was ready, we sat close against the fire. The thick liquid from the bowls burned all the way down, and I knew that by tomorrow my tongue would be blistered. Still, I continued to take large gulps, mixing it with the fine meat and tomato of the sandwiches.

The wood smoke rose, then drifted along the ground toward the river. We kept piling the damp brambles onto the flames. "Let's put a good share of wet branches on," Agnes said. "Then we can go off for a walk and come back and still have fire enough for more tea."

"Would you rather go for a boat ride?"

"Where would we get a boat?"

"There's one down in the rushes. I'm sure that the owner is safe at home in the town."

"All right."

The boat was easily undone, and in a few minutes we were moving slowly toward the center of the stream, paddling furiously with our hands. There seemed to be little current. Agnes was right; the dam had taken the greater force from the river. The water was like polished glass.

"Would you like to go above the falls?" I cried.

"But there's no way. Not even the boatmen go into that part."

"Let's try, then. We can cross the falls."

"I'm telling you, Thady, we won't make it."

I had often heard my father talk about the river above the falls. He had spoken of it in awe, saying that perch as big as salmon were to be had there, and that within the undergrowth and reeds of the bank were otters as fierce as mad dogs. It was all speculation, of course, since he had never been inside the natural garrison himself. He had seen shadows and heard stories. I decided to give it a try.

We were nearing the line of falls. I could feel the surge of the water beneath us as the white-headed rocks threw spray in our direction. Direct assault did not seem to be the answer. The water would only spin the boat around and perhaps overturn us. There was a flaw somewhere. There had to be. It needed only to be thought out, I told myself. I watched the currents.

146

The main flow ran through a canal close to the left bank of the river. At that point the channel was deep and treacherous. But what of the long garrison of rocks from that point outward? The spray was everywhere, like a fighting plume. Was it all show and bravado? How deep could the water be below? I asked myself.

I said nothing to Agnes but steered the boat toward the spray. She looked back at me several times, yet said nothing. Soon the mist enveloped us. It seemed to storm and rant like an animal. We were almost at the rim. Without warning, I jumped from the boat. Agnes screamed. As I had guessed, the water, though strong in force at this point, came only to my waist. The ground beneath me was sandy.

"We can easily get the boat over. I'll shove from this side. You just paddle when I tell you."

"No, Thady, I'm frightened. I think we should go back."

"What?"

"Please, love . . ."

Her eyes showed terror. My God, I thought, the most we could get was a good wetting. There was no fear of a mishap. I could have explained every detail to her, and yet she would have sat there petrified. If I had gone on, she would have undoubtedly been convinced in a matter of seconds. But something would have been lost. A word. A promise. An unspoken reliance. I pushed the boat away from the falls and swam after it. Once close to the shore, I managed to climb back in without too much difficulty.

"I'm sorry, Thady, if I ruined everything for you, but I'm in dread of water like that."

"That's okay."

"No, it isn't. You wanted to go over there more than anything. I could see that."

"Listen. I'll get Finn to do it with me someday when I come back. Then we'll tell you all about the fairy places over there."

"All right. But thank you for bringing me in."

As we paddled lazily along the shallows, I looked at the section of land and water across the falls. The woods seemed darker there, the sky more ominous above the black water. It was the center of Plassey, and we were merely floating on its outer periphery. The town, Mount Shannon, the woods, Sandy, the river, the falls, and at the heart's very core, this dark untouched place. My mind began to visualize the decreasing spirals. And in manipulating the small mathematics of my imaginary diagram, I thought that beyond the center the links of the spiral begin again. The old riddle of the dog and how far he can go into the wood. What then were the corresponding points moving out from the dark core? Dooneas, Castleconnel, Galway, Tuam. But what if the core were shifted to another perspective? Then Plassey with its memories and secrets would become outer and no longer inner. Would lose all meaning. Would cease to exist. It was all a focusing of the mind's eye. A choosing again that which pleases to know, but more importantly, that which delights to not know. I would have to jumble the lot if I were to go on, if I were to leave this place forever. But I reminded myself that I was going to stay. There would be little need to change anything.

The angelus bell was ringing as we tied the boat back in place. We found the fire red. The new tea took only minutes to make, and we ate every morsel of the remaining food. I sat close against the fire. Agnes turned my trousers back and forth in an effort to dry them by the warm rocks.

We made our way back through the woods, and by taking a small boreen avoided passing close to Mount Shannon House. The car was as we had left it. The drive back to the city took only minutes, as most of the day's traffic had cleared. The town had settled down to its routine of walks and pictures and variety shows.

I dropped Agnes off at her door. She thanked me. "I had

a wonderful time," she said. "I only hope that there will be more."

"There will."

"I won't be able to see you tomorrow because of work. I'm taking Bridie's shift as well as my own. But the next night? Could you come then?"

"That'd be fine. I'll be looking forward."

The sky was still bright as I parked the car in Higher Brazil Street. Our kitchen windows were lit, a candle for the dead burning in each one. I pushed open the door. There was no one in the kitchen. I sat in the large chair and leaned back. A little rest before supper would be nice, I told myself.

"Thady, you're home!" My mother's voice startled me. She was standing in the doorway. "I was just down for the milk. I didn't see you drive in."

"I just pulled up."

"What a lovely car. I'm glad you rented it."

"Why's that?"

"Well, the man was here from the solicitor's office. They want us up there tomorrow. I'll be glad when it's all over with."

She went immediately to the kitchen to prepare supper. I hurried to my room and changed clothes. I did not wish her to begin questioning me on the day's events.

After supper, sitting by the fire, I thought of the afternoon at Plassey and the warm but puzzling closeness of Agnes. I had not in my wildest ruminations expected such a reaction on her part. I had heard every excuse under the sun from cheap tramp to glib socialite. But here was a girl who merely asked to be treated like a human being and not—how was it she put it?—"plied like an old piano." Not even Jennifer, my wife, had known the reasoning behind her high and mighty attitude on sex. She would not, could not, she'd said, sleep with me before we were engaged. It was an assertion below her very will. But all other sexual antics were perfectly all right, part of the game that forbade only the quirk—intercourse. She could not explain her stand. She would not be moved from it. And she would hear no more argument. Her morality was of the same fiber as that total lack of control described by Agnes. I was just as guilty myself. Agnes belonged to a time I had known briefly as a teen-ager here in Ireland. Not that all the girls were models of purity and demanding of respect; rather was it that we, the boys, saw them in that light, and they became, almost by that estimate alone, worthy of admiration. How strange it was that as a young man I had despised those who broke that feminine virtue and prided themselves on the fact. But then, of course, for all my virtue, I had only seen the letter of the law, unable in my childish mind to put the focus on it that Agnes had done. I had lived by the polarities, and not for one instant had I understood the real intent of the law.

17

Thady

ON THURSDAY AFTERNOON, my mother, Sadie, and I drove to the lawyer's office in Perry Square. Kevin would meet us there, as he had dole cards to turn in at the labor exchange. We stood outside the tall Georgian doorway with its brass plate. *Mr. Patrick J. Rundon, Solicitor.* Impressive. Impassive, too. My mother and sister showed signs of nervousness as though they were about to enter into the presence of some supreme person. I banged on the door. "Oh, my God, Thady, not so loud," my mother said.

"It's just a lawyer's office."

"Come on now, love. Don't be showing off. Not today."

"Jesus, will all of you be under everyone's and anyone's

thumb for the rest of your lives? You pay him. He is your servant. Not ..."

The door opened. A young country girl ushered us into the hall. She seemed capable only of indifference. She called to some friends of hers who were picking their hair inside a glass sliding window. *Quinlan. Yes. Mr. Rundon was to see these people. Oh, he's not in yet.* My mother made some apology and said that we would be glad to wait. I tried to interrupt, but she waved me aside. She found a seat and left me in the center of the hall feeling foolish. When I reached her and Sadie, I whispered, "What did you do that for? We had an appointment. Are you just going to sit there and be insulted?"

"Thady, sit down," my mother commanded. "You can't make any fuss in places like this or they'll ignore you. These people are very learned, and they come and go as they please. Just look over there in that other room. There are people waiting longer than ourselves. Have some respect."

"Some respect? He's the one without respect. My position is equal to his, any day."

"These people are different than us. They're educated and have high appointments. We're not the same as ..."

"I'm not educated? I'm just a tramp who came in off the street?"

"Hush!"

At that moment the hall door opened and Kevin entered. He came over to the seat and asked if we had seen the solicitor yet. When told the story, he just shook his head and said, "Jesus!" He went outside again.

I sat back against the hard seat. Inside the glass, girls were taking their tea break. Their loud laughter circled the room, falling on the cowed heads of the old men and uneasy women waiting all about. A man in a raincoat shook his head in annoyance when I caught his eye. He shifted his position against the wall and turned away. I heard others complain and tell yarns of how they had waited several hours on previous days, only to

---

152

find that the lawyer had decided not to come at all because of the rain. Some predicted that he was at the seaside and might not come at all today. The phone rang several times, but no one answered. It was tea break. Their world had stopped.

I got up and opened the door. Kevin was sitting on the steps smoking. I sat beside him. His look of disgust told me that we were of a mind. "It's disgraceful, isn't it?" he said.

"I thought that it was only at the dispensary, long ago, that they were able to get away with that?"

"It's everywhere. You'd want to knock every one of them on their arse to wake them up. But then they'd put you in jail. They have you every way."

In his mad way he was right. I thought of the long lines at the dispensary, as a child, waiting for the free medicine. The smell of piss. The sauntering of the doctors past, as people fell aside like feudal serfs. The shouting of surnames at the collection window as though they were obscenities. No wonder the Irish exaggerated. If they didn't, the world would completely ignore them; but, more importantly, even their own would forget their existence.

I got up. Kevin looked frightenedly in my direction. Through the door. I ignored my mother and sister and made straight for the window. The tea break was finishing. A girl was answering the phone. *Yaas. Noo. He's not in yet. Yaas. Noo.* I banged on the window. The girl on the phone came toward me, stopping to pick up her cup on the way. The slide opened.

"Yaas?" she intoned in her affected accent.

"When will Mr. Rundon be in?"

"We're not sure. Wait over . . ."

"Wait, hell! My name is Mr. Thaddeus Quinlan. I had an appointment with your solicitor this afternoon . . ."

"I can't help . . ."

"You'll help it, by God, when I take our family account out of this dirty stable. I want to see your office manager immediately."

153

"What?"

"The man in charge when your errant employer is not around."

"You mean Mr. Tidings?"

"Get him now. I have never in my life witnessed such inefficiency. Or such a conglomeration of asinine peasants gathered together in one place."

It worked. More than the fury, the bite of the words took hold. Glares arose from desks, but heads went back to their keyboards. An amazing rhythm of typing began to replace the careless chatter. I heard doors slam. People behind me began to cough delightedly. My mother was talking furiously to the man who had nodded before. But he was laughing in her face. "Oh, Jesus," I heard her say.

More doors shutting. The glass partition behind the busy typists quivered. First the girl came through the quaking door, her face resentful. She was followed by an elderly man in a gray striped suit. He came immediately to the kiosk window.

"Mr. Quinlan?"

"Mr. Tomkins?"

"Tidings. May I help you, sir? There seems to have been some misunderstanding?"

"Only in the matter of an appointment which your Mr. Rundon seems to have forgotten."

"Ah, yes. My apologies." His voice lowered, in confidence. "You see, our Mr. Rundon is not the most punctual, you might say. It seems that we are in the midst of the horse showing in Dooradoyle. And, being an equestrian, he cannot resist the temptation to skip off between the courthouse and here to see some of his old friends who are in town for the occasion."

"Horses?"

"Heavens, no, Mr. Quinlan. You do have the Irish sense of humor."

"Ha."

"Well, in the meantime, here we are. If you wouldn't mind,

154

Mr. Quinlan, I can read your late father's will in Mr. Rundon's place."

"Will?"

"Yes. Your father did not die intestate."

What could this mean? "Very well, then. If you would read the will. The quicker the better."

My mother heard his words. She said nothing. We followed the gray gentleman into a large dark office which was bordered by shelves laden in rolled brown scrolls, piled carelessly upon each other. In the corner, a heap of the same documents gathered dust on the floor. Never in my life had I witnessed such disarray. The desk, too, was cluttered in ledgers, scraps of paper, and electrical wiring which ran in every direction. I thought of my lawyer's office in Nebraska. The clean mahogany desk. The pert, almost too efficient secretaries. No nonsense.

Mr. Tidings, having seated my mother in a soft chair and Sadie across from her on the sofa, beckoned to Kevin and me. "You may both sit on the couch, if you care to," he said. "However, it won't take very long. You may stand if you wish. Times were when these matters were so very formal. Progress. Progress."

"Yes," I said. "We'll stand."

Mr. Tidings did not look up from his desk again for several minutes. First he pored over some ledgers, and I saw him mouth the name Quinlan and the date 1940. That date was perhaps the time of my father's first business with the firm. From the books he took some correspondence which directed him to a sheaf of pages within his desk. He glanced over these, shuffling and reshuffling until a torn document was fished out. This he placed to his right. He rose from his desk without a word and stepped in the direction of the pile of manila envelopes in the corner. One after another of the folders was opened, examined, and replaced in the chaotic mound. Kevin cursed under his breath. Sadie made a tight face. My mother alone was calm and patient.

After a longer search, he suddenly exclaimed, "Ah, here it is. I knew I put it back just yesterday. Now we can get started."

He looked solemnly at all of us. His eyes assumed the cold stare of the solicitor he was not. He said very seriously as he tore open the seal, "Shall I proceed, with your permission?"

"Yes. By all means, do," I said.

"Yes, sir," my mother cried, turning a scowl in my direction.

He reared back like an eagle assuming full stature. The tiny pince-nez perched right on the point of his nose. I thought of a Dickensian character. A name suitable to the profession. Tidings. Of great joy. Which seldom are, in these premises. He began.

"The late Mr. Quinlan's affairs are uncomplicated. The will provides for yourself, Mrs. Quinlan, and for each of your children." He paused to adjust his collar. "To be brief, the property at 3 Higher Brazil Street, which has no liens and is free and clear, goes to Mrs. Quinlan. And a sum of one hundred pounds each to Thaddeus, Patrick, Madeline, Sarah, and Kevin Quinlan. These sums are at present in Mr. Quinlan's account at the Munster Provincial."

He removed his pince-nez.

"That's all?" I said.

"Quite," Tidings replied. "You realize, of course, that had the deceased died intestate, the inheritance would have, under the Succession Act, approximated its present terms."

"When was this will drawn?"

"Over two months ago."

"Was this the total of my father's estate—five hundred pounds and the house property?"

"No, Mr. Quinlan. The estate was closer to several thousand pounds. However, the deceased, several months before his death, liquidated the greater amount of his assets."

"Where, then, are the monies?"

"I regret to say this, but they went to several Catholic charities. I am not a Catholic myself, but I believe that masses and such took a great part of the sums."

"You mean that my father in his sane mind gave practically everything he owned to the Church?"

"The question of sanity, Mr. Quinlan, is a matter of opinion. The deceased was, at the time he issued those checks, extremely upset and distraught. I believe that, a day or so before, he had come to realize how little time he had to live."

"He knew exactly?"

"He did."

"Jesus Christ!"

My mother was the first to break the silence. She moaned, "Oh, Jesus, save us!" Sadie went to her side. Kevin was nervously scratching his back. Mr. Tidings asked if he could get us some tea, and, when no one accepted, offered us his office for as long as we wished, to gain our composure. If we needed him, all we had to do was touch the bell on his desk. We thanked him and he left.

The game was over at last. The final caper revealed. The great joke, a sad one for the player and all of the played, except myself. Through the thunder and flashing of antlers my father had come down to nothing but a frightened man. All the songs and words and fires were mere illusions. All the bravado as empty as a spoiled sepulchre. But the pain and death of compassion were very real to my mother and sister. I watched them console each other. They had been cheated of that which we had come to regard as a natural right. But more than the myth of self-to-family-to-race-to-humanity, they saw now the only vital bond discarded and sneered at. The bond of friendship. Their obligation to him had ended years before, when, instead of being the giant of all he surveyed, he had become an old toothless dog whose snarls are tolerated. They could judge him now but wouldn't, because their ways forbade it. But I, who owed him nothing except the very severance that set me free, could see his guilt, and yet, being so like him myself, would have to beg off on any judgment. I tried to imagine my father making his awful decision in our kitchen with my mother preparing his food and Sadie washing his clothes. Could he have taken a pen right there and cut himself off from human feeling? I doubted if he could have done that. Rather had he contrived to disinherit by feigning this paltry inheritance. He had come to this stranger's office and commissioned this impartial lackey to arrange the proper but artificial words of deceit. Not his own words, but staid and blunt terms used by both high and low alike in their common dealings.

What galled me more than anything else was that for this final abandonment to self he would be spoken of as a giant by his cronies and priests alike. What sort of human society is it that sneers at the plight of other living things and calls selfishness and indulgence true virtue? A man of the Church, they would say. A firebrand! A terrible man! And it all utter nonsense. The reality of the tormented man without hope would never be known. The human soul tortured by memories of drudgery and goaded by medieval threats of eternal damnation would never be discussed for fear that the bravado would die and with it the fantasy that, though the world rejected them, the Irish were indeed the children of God. They would never face up to life, if they lived a thousand years. Inside their souls was the land of Faery. Outside was dire peasant ignorance and poverty. There never had been and never would be a middle ground of hope. For one man alone, Bernard Mary Quinlan, I would see to it that the myth died with the man, that the normal antics of heart and head were kept at even keel and never allowed to abscess into fantasy.

I went across to my mother. She had stopped crying at this

point and was staring straight ahead. Sadie showed concern and did not betray her own disappointment.

"Let's go," I said. "Let's get out of here."

My mother stood and hung heavily on my shoulder. Sadie was close beside me as we walked through the lobby and into the street where Kevin was leaning against the iron grating. I helped my mother to the car. Sadie sat with her in the back seat. Kevin did not join us. I went across to him.

"Aren't you coming with us?"

"No. I'm fucking pissed off and fed up. The dirty . . ."

"What are you going to do?"

"Go off and get langared drunk, I would, if I had a pound."

"I'll loan you a few quid."

"Would you, Thaed? I'll pay you back when I get the dole."

"Just don't mention one word of what's happened to anyone."

"No, I won't. Oh, God, I won't."

"I have your word?"

"You do."

I reached in my pocket and found several notes. I gave him five pounds. His eyes lit up. He thanked me from the bottom of his heart, he said, and was gone off somewhere.

Back at the car the two women sat close together. "You're too good, Thaed," Sadie said. "But you should not have given him any money. He'll just drink it." She looked nervously at my mother.

"That's why I gave it to him. We could all do with a couple of drinks right now."

"But that's it, Thady. Haven't you noticed it about him? It won't stop at a few. He's a martyr for the drink. He's afflicted with the curse . . ."

"Ah, he's not," my mother retorted. "Don't be saying

---

things you don't mean. He likes a couple of drinks like any man."

" 'Man'?" Sadie cried. "A man is one who goes out and earns his keep. A worker. And 'a few drinks'? Jesus help us! He'd drink Loch Erin dry."

"Are you serious?" I said. "I thought that the drink was all part of the funeral and the upset."

"Would to God that it was! He's a bloody . . ."

"Enough!" my mother said. "That's enough! I'll hear no more against him."

I remembered Paddy's advice to Kevin. He had not been making idle conversation with his younger brother. I remembered, too, my own promise to Paddy, made partly in fun.

My mother touched my coat with her hand, and I knew that a long chain had begun. That my father's austerity and selfishness had created these wards who would need my attention. Though made of the same fiber as him, I could not flee this time and fabricate a mesh of comfortable anger.

"I want neither of you to divulge even the slightest detail of what went on in the solicitor's office today," I said. "Not even to Maud. Let it suffice for her to know only that she will receive a hundred pounds. Say nothing about the rest. Is that clear?"

"Yes," they said together.

"That's settled then?"

"It is."

18

Thady

ON FRIDAY AFTERNOON, William Street was more crowded and congested than I had remembered it to be years before. With no small difficulty, I found a parking space near the Rialto Theatre where as schoolboys we often hid from the keen eyes of the parading Brothers in the primary school yard across the street. The theatre was closed now, but the same strips of black tape covered the breasts and crotches of the actresses lounging in their sun-filled bills. Once we had opened the glass cases and removed the tapes. It was all a game to lure us on—the ladies were decently dressed underneath. I stood now and surveyed the old school. The gray dark walls gave no indication of life within. Occasionally a black Brother drifted out of a door, but just as suddenly disappeared. I felt the same apprehension that I had felt on cold winter mornings, standing shivering outside the railings in my short and worn trousers, without a morsel in my stomach.

I walked through the outer yard. Along the sides, flower gardens had been planted, and the early plants brightened the drabness of the grounds. Through the small stile and into the secondary's compound. To the left the jakes were still gushing their cleansing fluid. Two boys were urinating and carrying on a lively conversation. I remembered all the cigarette breaks taken down there. The jokes told. The girls seduced, in word only. I walked into the center yard and faced the monastery house.

The door buzzer rang through what seemed a hollow shell. I waited for a response. At first, nothing. Then the closing of a door deep inside. Another, louder sound. The door within the glass vestibule opened, revealing a dark mahogany hall. A pert country maid undid the latch and smiled. I said that I had an appointment with Brother Cleary, the headmaster. She seemed to know all about it and said that I should make myself comfortable in the parlor. She took my coat. I was ushered into a spacious room off the main hall. Then she was gone.

I sat in a black leather chair close to the fireplace. The room, despite its vaultlike appearance, was quite cozy. On the walls hung portraits of past superiors of the monastery, their solemn faces seeming to pry into the darkest corners of the room. Above the mantel was a painting of Edmund Tracey, the founder of the Saint Joseph Brothers. He was smiling at some distant mission on the painted horizon. I had always liked his kind face. I liked this room, too, and could visualize long chats by the hearth on winter nights.

Through the house I could hear the velvet bells calling various Brothers to their prayers and duties. *One bell, Brother John. Two bells, Brother Stephen.* Secret names, since their order used only surnames to the outside world. *Brother Thadde*

. . . The door opened, breaking my reverie. A tall, robust man came toward me and grabbed my hand. "How are you, Thady?" he said. "It's a pleasure, indeed, to meet you."

"Thank you, Brother. My pleasure, too."

"Isn't it strange weather, thank God, for this time of year? One day we have the sun, and we're scorched. The next it's cold rain, and we're huddled comfortably by the fire. That's what I call lovely—not knowing what to expect. How about you?"

"The same, Brother."

"None of that *Brother* stuff. You're not over in the dusty halls anymore. Sean Cleary is me name and fame. Call me Sean."

"Sean, then."

"Grand. Can I get you a little brandy? I'm going to have one myself."

"Well, if you're going to, Brother. I mean Sean."

"Right with you in a jiffy."

I watched him pour the fine amber liquid. Little had I realized when I was a boy here that I would one day be taking strong drink with my master. The years away had paid off.

"There you are, Thady. And here's health to you."

"Thank you, Broth . . . Sean."

"Now you're getting the hang of it."

"It's hard at first."

"Just like everything, Thady. It was hard, I'll bet, too, when you left the safety of this old place and went out into the cold world."

"It wasn't easy."

"I was there myself. I worked as a docker in England for many a year before I dreamed of becoming a Brother. And there are times when I feel that maybe I took the soft road, coming into the order. We sometimes set up cozy little worlds for ourselves, and it's hard getting out of them. Couldn't you imagine the headlines if I up and left this place? 'Saint Joseph Brother Leaves Order to Resume Old Job as Docker.' "

He roared with laughter. His bright eyes kindled at the prospect. But I thought that I detected a sad note in his voice, as if the back of his mind harbored a deep longing for the honest dirt and mire of his old self. He could never go back. He knew that. I wondered perhaps if there had been women. I thought of my night on the docks. Had he known them, or kept his holy distance?

"Well, Thady, tell me about yourself, and all the things that have happened to you since you scourged us here." He smiled.

"All?"

"All that's decent."

The brandy loosened my tongue, or so I thought. I told him of my father's angry words. Of my retreat. He nodded as though he knew it all to be part of a mosaic, a natural expectation. I spoke of England. Of the days as a messenger in New York. The air force. And I found myself beginning to talk about Jennifer. As though edging cautiously, but honestly, through a precarious confession, I began to tell all that had happened. On occasion I skipped over small details, but the man in front of me was too knowing and sincere to be deluded. I went back over my story and filled in the painful explanations. I blamed my own ambition, my lack of understanding, my inability to cope with another person's needs, and my blind drive to prove to my father that I was capable of success without him. It all poured out in a stream so turbulent as to amaze me. I had needed this moment for years. I didn't care about the consequences. I was my own man at last, standing on my faults, if nothing else.

When I finished, Brother Cleary brought the decanter to the fireside and filled my glass and his. "Will you stay for tea?" he said.

"I can't refuse. Not with that grand smell of scones coming through the walls."

"You have a good nose for food. Like my own. I can catch the whiff of supper as far down as Patrick Street." He went toward the door and pressed a small buzzer on the wall. "She'll be in any minute now. We'll just have time for our brandies."

He settled himself into his chair. I knew that he was going to discuss the position. I placed my brandy on the fireside table.

"Thady," he said. "I don't have to tell you that your credentials are in order. And how you got them is important, too. It's not as if you sat on your duff and let your parents or a benevolent government hand-feed you, as we say. No. There's no problem there. However, and I feel ashamed to have to say this, there are some things that present a stumbling block. Mind you, they don't hinder the educational possibilities, but they do hinder such chances *in Ireland*. And that's a cat of a different color."

"How do you mean?"

"Well, Thady, take the least first. You haven't a dog's notion of Irish, do you? I mean of the language or the legends? Not so much that you don't have a notion, really, but that you would not be able to *teach* Irish. Would you now?"

"I wouldn't."

"There you are, and I'll admit it's a small thing, but it's there in black and white. You must have a speaking and writing knowledge of the language. And a certificate to prove it."

"But the children are versed in English. I would be teaching English, wouldn't I?"

"You would. But you'd still have to have that certificate."

"Could I work toward one and teach in the interim?"

"Not here. In Dublin, yes. But it would take a full course at a teachers' college."

"How long would that take?"

"A year, at least, but . . ."

"That's a tall order, but I have a little money. I should . . ."

"There's more, Thady, I'm sorry to say."

"What?"

"You see, you didn't have to tell me this afternoon about

your marriage. I knew. The superior here had a full report. I argued your side, but he's a country man, and God bless him, he has never been out of Ireland in his life. He thinks that there's only one way. And that's the old one. He wouldn't hear of your appointment, Thady. I'm sorry."

"Where did he get this information?"

"From some wagging tongue. There are many of those around."

"Probably one of my own, more than likely."

"I wouldn't doubt it."

"By the way then, what of this Englishman who's on your staff? Isn't he an outsider? And a Protestant? What does he think of him?"

"I brought that up in your defense. His words were very hard."

"Yes?"

"He said that heretics were one thing, but apostates were quite another story."

"An apostate?"

"Yes, Thady, if you take Saint Paul's narrow mind for your basis. But that includes all of us who went off the beaten track. I'm dreadfully sorry. I can never act as judge. I'm always weighing the possibilities. I'll make a poor superior when my day comes around."

"I don't think so."

These words that described my spiritual condition were terrifying. It was being declared officially an outcast. Made alone by the edict of some anointed one. Cast out from the fold. Cursed. Branded. Pronounced dead by Divine Godhead.

Brother Cleary must have sensed my distress, as he began to speak of his days in England and the wild times he had had before coming into the cassock and soutane, as he put it. Gradually, I found the anxiety leave me. The warm tea and scones, when they were brought, helped, too. We spoke of old days at the school and the wild times past. On and on we went, laughing and matching each other in yarns.

Outside it began to darken, and I knew that I must go if I was to make the ticket office before closing. I thanked Brother Cleary for his kindness. He made me promise that if I ever came back again, I would look him up first before anybody else. He clutched my hand tightly and wished me good luck.

I crossed the yard quickly. As I unlatched the outer gate, I turned and looked back. He was standing in the archway where I had left him. He waved. But I did not wave back.

19

Agnes

IT WAS LATE on Friday afternoon and no sign nor light of Thady. Bridie had not yet arrived to relieve me, and I spent my time arranging the pewter mugs behind the bar. Of course, Thady hadn't said anything about the time he'd be in. I just thought that he knew the time I got off. Maybe I was expecting too much, I said to myself. It was like the other day up Plassey, when I expected Thady to be a golden knight and whisk me off my feet. Instead, beneath the fine clothes and scent, I found him no different than any other man, and even a little more forward and impatient. But, God forgive me, I found myself liking that more than the fairy tale I had had of him.

Bridie was only a few minutes late. I stayed and talked to her to see if Thady would make it. She tried to hint about our picnic up Plassey, but I evaded her questions, saying that I'd tell her all the details another time. This only whetted her appetite for information. She kept probing me, trying to establish a picture of our date that would liven her bright notions over the cold nights. Bridie was nearly thirty-five and had no prospects of a lover.

As I was about to go home, Finn Keough came bursting through the door. His face was flustered and perspiring. "Have you seen Thady?" he shouted.

"No. I thought that he might be with you."

"He's nowhere to be found."

"He's not at home?"

"They're looking for him too. He was to see the Brothers about that job, this afternoon."

"I know. Well, the news may have been good, and he went to have a few drinks to celebrate."

"You know, Agnes, you have a point there. I'll bet he got the bloody thing with flying colors, and he went into the Dunmartin and went on the tear."

The mention of the hotel stung me. All of Bridie's taunts about stylish women were, I knew, nonsense, but yet I was selfish enough to worry. But hadn't he been married? Hadn't she been a beautiful girl by the photographs Finn showed around at the time? She had been an American, and I supposed that like all of them she was fresh and spotless and perfumed beyond a flaw. If he had known her and still saw fit to touch me, then I must count for something to him. Why did I go on worrying myself like this? I was a shame to myself.

Finn was excited. "I'll bet that he'll be here in less than an hour. We'll get our coats on and paint this town from one end to the other. We'll dance on the roofs."

"If you say so."

"And Thady'll say so, too, after getting that job."

"But are you sure of the job?"

"Certainly. Listen, I'll tell you what. Let me buy you a drink to sip on. Then I'll go in search of Thady. I'll surely meet him coming down the street. We'll drop by his house to give them the good news, and then we'll be back down here."

I had a small sherry, and Finn left in search of Thady. God Almighty, I said to myself, I hope nothing has happened to him this night. I felt helpless. Somehow, I knew that the job had fallen through. He was down and would need the time to come to himself. I could not move toward him without his consent.

Bridie brought me another sherry but did not say a word. She knew that something was wrong and had put aside her romantic notions. For all her wild ideas, where would I be without her? If I was not like her entirely, what indeed was it that I now expected out of the future? What could I expect of the last few happy days? I could say without a lie on my tongue that I wanted a small light to burn in my life. I hoped that Thady would come again and that I would count the days until he arrived. And then when he left, as he must, I would begin again the expectation. I hoped that every now and again the postman would bring me a letter that said Thady Quinlan was alive and well and that on a dark night he had thought of me and wished me near. I hoped that Finn and I would sit and talk of Thady as one talks of the blackbird in flight and waits for it to alight nearby, never daring to trap it, lest its feathers come apart in the hand.

What an amadan you are, Agnes Gilligan, I told myself. Dreaming like a little child. Putting lights in the darkness where they were never meant to be. I would have to face up to my sorrows. I would have to make a life for myself. This day-to-day hoping would never do. And I was tired of being nothing to nobody.

Bridie tried to pour me another drink, but I refused. I would walk awhile and think of all the possibilities that lay ahead. The wind was fresh on my face as I left the pub by the side door. The trees shook their drops of moisture loose as I passed beneath them. I would turn back soon when all was quiet.

170

20

Thady

I RETURNED the rented car to Punch's Cross and took the bus back into the city. At the ticket office a clerk assured me of a seat on the *Saint Brendan*. He was telling lies, of course. There were seldom seats at this time of year. But I said nothing.

Matthew Bridge was deserted as I crossed it on my way back home. A lone bicycle coming off the hill approached me with its wavering light. I paid little attention as it passed, but suddenly behind me there was a loud roar of recognition. Finn Keough. "Thady Quinlan! Where in the name of Jesus have you been? I've been looking for you all over to celebrate your good fortune. You did get the job?"

"I didn't."

"What the holy fuck!"

"I didn't get the job. I wasn't suited to their standards."

"What?"

"I'll tell you at the house."

"Hop on."

"On the bike?"

"Of course."

Away we went up the hill. Then down through Athlunkard Street with its twinkling of lights and small shop windows closing their shades for the evening. Dogs barked at us from the curb. Small children waved to Finn as we had done ourselves years before when certain madmen happened upon us in the early evening. The light was fading fast from the sky. It would be pitch black over the church in a matter of an hour, and the long night would begin. I felt the tears stream down my face as we rumbled over the old stones. Finn didn't notice, and I was glad of that.

The house was flooded in light as we approached 3 Higher Brazil Street. My mother was at the door. "Lord, Thady," she said. "We thought that you went back to America without saying good-bye." Then there was laughter. She continued, "We have more than one celebration this evening. Isn't little Gerard there after getting an appointment to the *Post and Telegraph.* He'll start right when the summer begins. Isn't that great now? Well, tell us all about your success. We're dying to hear."

I looked around the room. Gerard was against the mantel, and when my eyes caught his he looked away. He was ashamed of what had been decided for him, I knew. I would try to turn the tide for him later with words to Maud, but now I had to face my own judges. They were all about, anticipating the failure that they would remember forever. Sadie at the table. Maud, serious, almost scowling, by the fireplace.

"There was no success."

"What, love? What are you saying?" My mother's voice at high pitch.

"I simply didn't get the job."

"Did your education come against you? There, I told you, there's no knowing to the high standards they ask for here."

"Oh, nonsense! There were other matters."

"Your marriage?"

"Yes."

"Oh, Jesus, Mary, and Joseph," she cried. "Why did you have to mention that to them?"

"They knew, and anyway, I wanted it to be known."

"You wanted a disgraceful thing like that divorce out in the open for all to sneer at?"

"Sneer at? For the love of God, Mama, every man jack in this country would be divorced if he had his way, and all you bloody women know it. I was divorced because I never should have been married in the first place. No Irishman is fit to be married. His whole upbringing—the want, the starvation of every human desire, the tyranny of country mugs posing as true priests, make him an unfit animal in any civilized society. He goes around in a bloody dream all his life, because he's afraid to give himself to anything."

"Your father . . ."

"My father?"

"Our father was a good strong man," Maud cried. "Let no one say anything against him. He was hard on us, but he was a good father and husband. And if he *did* give everything to the Church, we should be proud . . ."

I turned on my mother. "You told her," I said. "After I gave you strict instructions not to say a word to anybody."

"She drew it out of me," my mother said. "And anyway, Thady, what's the harm if people know?"

I looked at Finn. He had heard the comment clearly. He could not be expected to keep quiet. It was as it had always been. Nothing could be contained.

I took my place at the kitchen table. Gerard was by the fire now. The others had begun to move about the room, making small busy noises. Finn was accepting a pint of stout from my mother. I spoke across to Gerard. "Will there be no more school for you now?" I said.

"I suppose not," he replied.

"Not even at night?"

"There's only the technical school at night. No secondary or university level."

"Wasn't there a chance of a scholarship to U.C.D.? Didn't somebody mention that?"

"Yes. I had a good chance."

"But why this, then?"

He did not reply, but dropped his head deep into his shoulders. He was uneasy under my stare. Still only a child for all the knowledge. Maud had heard the conversation. She was coming across.

"Don't be putting wild ideas into his head now." She laughed with bitterness, the cup of tea in her hand shaking. "That's all right for ye over there in America to treat yourselves like gods, but we have to make our bread from day to day. A plumber's son has no place being in the university. His place is to get himself a secure job and raise a family. Deal o' good your education has done you. You can't even get a job in your own town."

"Maybe you're right," I said. "But would you ever consider letting him come to the States? He could work and finish school too."

I did not expect the violence that came into her mood. "Go on out," she said to Gerard. "Go on outside."

He arose. As he passed his mother, she caught him by the arm and led him to the doorway. She slammed the door behind him. I was curious to see what all this was leading up to. I did not have long to wait. She whirled on me without warning.

"I have only a few words for you, Thady," she said. "Hear

---

them and hear them good. Now, I have heard nothing for the last week from that child but your conversation with him about art this and art that. You have turned his mind by making him seem important, more important than the child he is. We're not trying to hold him back. But first things come first. And as for your offer to take him over, well, you can knock that in the head right now. If I was on my dying bed, I would prevent him from going there. A country where there is no morality. Where everyone is as selfish as the next. A godless, impure place. No, Thady Quinlan, you're at home there, but then you'd be at home anywhere, because you've cut yourself off from everything and anything. But my son, or any flesh of mine, will never set foot on that cursed soil."

"For the love of Almighty God will ye stop!" Sadie shouted. "A brother and sister talking to one another like that."

There was a long silence. Gerard came back in after awhile but sat at the other end of the room. I watched him. I knew that it had been a mistake to try and change the course of his destiny. He was condemned to spend his time with stamps and wax and gummed labels. In later years, perhaps, he might rise above his petty life and break the saddles laid upon him. But then again he might lean toward the inbred road of the provincial intellectual, vegetating by the pub fire, scorning those who ventured beyond the pale. I could not tell at this time. The balance between the extreme of madness and that of utter silence was his alone.

Maud and her family left early. Before going to the door, she came across and kissed me. "I'm sorry, Thaed," she said. "I say things that I don't mean half the time."

"Don't we all?"

"I don't want any bad blood between us."

"There won't be."

"I'll be down tomorrow."

"I'll see you then."

Gerard came across and shook my hand. He smiled bravely. "Would you write me, Uncle Thady?" he said.

"I surely will."

After several cups of strong tea, Finn said that we would have to go by Agnes's job to pick her up. "No, Finn," I said. "It wouldn't be fair."

"Fair to who and what? I told her I'd bring you by with any news."

"She won't have to be told. She'll know."

"But Thady, you can't ..."

"I must."

I knew that he did not understand, and I could never hope to explain. Somehow I felt that Agnes would understand. She would know how desperately we both needed the dream, but how empty it would leave us in the end. Perhaps, I thought, if we could learn to cope with the frailty of our affection and ... But I was dreaming. Like all the times before. I was playing with threads of words and fashioning them into a hopeless mirage.

Finn and I sat by the fire until early morning. The conversation was of old times. Finn would never change, nor want to. He knew in his heart that I would come back and that there would be a way, he said. He even promised to double his daily prayers for that order. I did not lie to him, but he refused to heed my argument. How did I know how I'd feel in a month or so? he insisted. This was my home.

He left around five o'clock. I read Jennifer's letter once again. It made me feel angry and sad all at once. But I knew what I had to do. We had to talk this matter over. There was so much to be considered when it came to our child, Bernie. So much.

21

Thady

AT AROUND SIX O'CLOCK (I had just heard the angelus bell ring) there was a commotion at the door. I left the small writing table to investigate. It was Kevin. I had not noticed his absence the previous night, nor had anybody else, it seemed. In the light of the lane he stood, or rather wavered, unable in his obvious drunkenness to undo the latch of the half door. I reached and pulled it open. For a moment his eyes just stared into the darkness. I was reminded of the small animals so often startled by my headlights on some deserted prairie road. I reached out and braced him. His body complied, allowing me to steer him through the obstacles of the kitchen and toward the red fire. "Thanks, Thaed," he managed as he fell into the armchair.

I poured him a mug of hot tea. The liquid seemed to revive him somewhat. His eyes began to focus, staring at me now from his young though mottled face.

"How's the goin', Thaed?" he said.

"Fine," I replied, holding back the urge to smile at his awkwardness.

"Good, good. Jasus, that's good. Is there any drop of drink around, do you think?"

"Not a drop in the house. Finn had the last stout."

"The bollocks! Them women! Serving strangers and leaving their own without. Bloody bitches of . . ."

I decided to let it pass. All we needed was another row on our hands. "Where in heaven's name were you till this hour, Kev?" I said.

The question tightened his face. Insolence, perhaps, I thought. But no, it was merely a searching for thoughts which would satisfy my inquiry and render me silent. "Ah, a wild night. Like every Friday night. Piss drunk we got, me and the lads. Thrown out of four public houses." The details were meant to impress, I knew.

He began to doze. I quickly shook him, saying, "Why don't you get your boots off, Kevin. And your clothes. Before Mama and Sadie get up and find you."

This seemed to sour him. He looked into my face. "I'm all right," he said. "This is my house. There's no fear of me. None at all. I'm me own man and daren't . . ."

I moved back to my chair and watched him settle into sleep again. What was he? I thought. No more than twenty years old and already a sour, sodden drunk. Unable to keep a job, Paddy had said. Insulted at the suggestion of responsibility. A parasite the rest of his days, dependent upon the women, yet scorning their every word. I had known him only as a child. His growing to be a man a mystery to me, save for my mother's mention of his failings. Expelled from primary school. Not even the minimum education that would gain him the lowest of occupations. All the others would have dignity. But not Kevin. It would be hand to mouth to bowels to earth—a hopeless circle of shame and despair. And I was powerless to help him. It was the unalterable way of all we had come from, all that we were destined to be if we did not strike back and fly in its face.

And this brother that I knew only as a passerby knows a waif on the quays would grow to touch and maim all that lived about him. The women more than anybody. The women—Sadie, my mother, the poor misfortune he might choose to marry. A girl like Agnes. The thought unsettled me. But I knew that he and his likes would be her heritage and last hope. Only to leave her more destitute than before. And wasn't I, too, like him? Hadn't I been what he would be? Hadn't I married and used and not loved sufficiently Jennifer, my wife? Wasn't I of the same blood as he? Of the same blood as my father? That same dead blood, feeding its own decay? Telling myself that there was only me and nothing more. Carrying on the tradition I had told myself I despised. And with Agnes, didn't I owe her more than a dismissal? If I did not owe her a promise, did I not owe her the courtesy of a reason for my going? She was not like this heavy heap of human flesh before me. She was alive and warm, without carapace or façade. I could not leave in silence unless I was no more than the man who walked through that half door a week ago, I told myself. Had I learned nothing? Had the death and the spite and the deceit meant not one iota? It had. I knew it had.

I stepped over my prostrate brother. He stirred in his stupor. My coat was still on the stand. I threw it about me, tightening the neck button against the cold.

22

Thady

THE HOUSE at the corner of Sheep Street was in darkness. I looked across the Abbey common; not a soul moved anywhere. I tapped lightly on the door. To my surprise it was answered almost immediately, and there stood Agnes, fully dressed.

"Were you up?" I said.

"Oh, I just dozed off on the chair last . . ."

"I'm sorry. Everything fell apart. I didn't want to burden you with my troubles."

"Come in, Thaed. Come in. You'll catch your death out there in the damp."

I walked ahead of her into the small dark parlor. Everything in the room was arranged tidily, as I had guessed. A picture of a stern old woman above the mantel. Silver candlesticks on the dresser. A small table near the fireplace. A statue of Saint Jude on a marble stand.

"Sit down, Thaed. Will you have a cup of tea or coffee?"

"No, thanks. I can't stay long. I've been up all night. Finn isn't long gone. We talked all night."

"When do you have to go?"

"Today. The late train to Dun Leery."

"Oh, I see."

Her eyes fell. In the dim light I saw the soft flesh of her face tremble, but she gained control of herself and made to arrange the pillows on the chair beside her.

"There was no way, Agnes. They flatly refused to have me."

"In God's name, why?"

" 'An apostate,' the man said. One who believed and believes no more."

"Those awful villains! If it was only known. The stories that come out of that place. The twisted people they have in that order. And they having the nerve to condemn another human misfortune."

"It's all past now, and maybe they were right in the long run. I've been gone too long. I might only grow to despise the confinement."

"But another job. Wouldn't you try another line of work? There are a hundred new companies in the country. Foreign companies, some American. Surely . . ."

"No. It wouldn't work. I couldn't stay. I've grown apart."

"What will you do when you go back—go on teaching?"

"I have no reason not to. It's a good job, as Paddy would say. I'll be lost for awhile, but I'll pull out in my own direction. I'll make the best of it. And you?"

She answered as though she had anticipated the question. "The same as yourself, Thaed, I'll manage. I was thinking last night that there's nothing here for me. Being alive is more than the occasional happiness, it is finding some permanent well of that happiness and living close to it. I'm secure here, sure, but not very happy. Not as happy as I tell myself I am. Maybe when the summer comes I'll take my holidays in England and see if there is something I could do there. Something more than just slopping behind a pub counter. Something with a little importance to it. And maybe . . ." Her voice broke, and I saw the tears well up in her eyes.

"Maybe what?"

"Maybe nothing, Thaed."

"Your husband?"

"Yes. He's over there. He might have changed. There might be hope."

"Jesus Christ, don't say that! You know that that would be the death of you. You would sink into the mire like all the rest of them. You deserve more, Agnes. More than he has given or could give. More than this cursed bleak place can give. What kind of man would I be to let you do something like this, to stand by and not . . ."

"No, Thady, don't say it. I know it must be on your lips. I'd be a fool not to see it and want it. But don't say it. Say only that we had a grand time, that good things were felt, that we laughed and were angry all in the same day. Say only that. If you said more I would call it pity—and what more could I call it right now? All your sincerity could only come to that, now. But wait. Say what it is you have to say from over there. Say it from that place that is rightfully yours, that place where you will be the rest of your life. Say it from there, and I will not shut off your voice."

Her words stunned me. She was far stronger than I had given her credit for. She was above the filth and the stench and the tradition. Her stand was her own. I had mistaken toleration for complacency.

At the door I kissed her hard on the mouth. In the lee of

my arms she looked so small and frail. But she held me so tightly that her fingers gouged my flesh.

"You must go now," she said. 'Get some sleep before that awful train tonight."

"Good-bye," I said as I turned.

"Good-bye, Thady Quinlan, and Godspeed to you."

Some women passing on their way to Saint Mary's first mass looked across at us. An older one in a shawl scowled, but her small squat companion smiled. They drifted off toward the ruined tenements, their chatter brightening the drab April day.

23

Thady

MY MOTHER, Maud, Sadie, and Kevin insisted on seeing me off at the station, but I refused. When the taxi arrived, I kissed them quickly and made all the usual promises, deciding to try to keep most of them. I could stay forever, they said. There was no earthly reason for me to leave. And they were right, in their way. I would eventually have landed a job of some order. But I knew that I could never again be part of here, or there, as I had been, but only part of where I functioned at the time, by my wit's or heart's command. Like the obstacles at a regatta, some small perimeters had been set, and I would, somehow, pilot or twist my way among them, caught up momentarily in their imposed and artificial intricacies. I would learn nothing, but only know more deeply what it was I had. I would balance each day's light with its darkness, calling all the places forth, but never caring to remember their names, save for the faces seen at their corners, as one sees the faces of children, at diner's windows, passing like white summer lightning through small stations and country towns. Summer would come, I knew. Nebraska would green and die in the instant of the smallest blinking. The smells of the beet mash on every shoe. I smiled at the thought as I entered the cab. A mongrel whelp was pissing against the rainspout of our house.

Finn moved over on the seat. The bags were safely piled by his shoes. My mother was crying in her apron. Sadie looked small and tiny. Maud was big and ripe with her child. Kevin just stared.

I ordered the hackney to drive fast so as not to miss the train. I did not look back.

Stepping from the cab at the station, I asked a man if the train was in. He was polite and took time to tell me of a rough crossing. He said that the train was on the platform and was as empty as a tomb. Everybody coming home for Easter, he said. Wouldn't it be lovely if we never had to leave at all? I simply nodded. And he scurried off down a foul lane to the warmth of coals that he had paid for from far away.

Finn carried the bags. The old ticket man was half-asleep behind his spectacles as he punched the tiny railway card and waved me into the steam and soot of Limerick Station. He pointed to Finn. "He can't go on the platform."

"This man is Thaddeus Quinlan, an American professor, and I'm his friend. And by Jesus if you don't open that gate I'll break your fucking head open." Finn's face like autumn fire.

The old collector was unabashed. Not the slightest sign of being intimidated. "I don't give a dog's bollocks who he is, or who you might be, or what you think you can do. You stay. He goes."

Finn dropped the cases. I saw his move and quickly

reached into my pocket. The hexagonal coin flashed in the light. The old man reached and covered it with his palm. He immediately opened the stile. Finn breathed hard but lifted the suitcases and walked ahead. The man locked the stile behind us.

I was aboard the train at last. Soon the shuntings began. The train was edging gradually toward the darkness outside. Finn was at his best. His voice like a child's at a Christmas recital. Rehearsed, but, nonetheless, as sincere as was possible. "May smooth juicy bacon protect you," he began. "May gatter as tight as mouse holes ever service your wishes. May cream as thick as mountains pour long into your tea. May a cauldron full of the grandest pottage ever grace your table. May a panful of big smelly sausage be always on your hearth. And may . . ."

"There's no hope for you, you crazy blackguard," I said. And he laughed loud and long.

The lights twinkle. Men in embroidered uniforms shout at one another and at the night. Last whistle. The jarring of the carriages to a smooth rhythmic sway. And, behind in the station, Finn's convulsive waving on the eternal platforms. A shop closing for the night. Where they sell coats of arms for a pound. Which I do not need on my way to the sea, and the gulls that call it home. I think of Agnes and wish that she were near me now.